She Saw
Something

An Artemis Blythe Mystery Thriller

Steve Higgs

CONTENTS

PROLOGUE

THE MOON CAST AN eerie glow upon the quiet, desolate street as the man known only as the soldier crept closer to his target. He moved with the precision and stealth of a predator stalking its prey. Eyes narrowed, he studied the apartment building that housed Artemis Blythe—a name he despised with every fiber of his being.

More so, he despised what she represented.

Happiness for Cameron Forester... the man who'd taken his damn limb.

The soldier's lip curled into a painful snarl, the scars on his cheeks stretching into a jack-o-lantern leer.

"Artemis Blythe," he whispered under his breath, savoring the syllables and the anticipation of what was to come. His voice was gravelly, menacing—an indication of the darkness that lurked within him.

The soldier was a tall figure, broad-shouldered and muscular, his movements lithe and fluid. His face was chiseled, sharp angles and cold eyes set beneath a furrowed brow. The skin on the left side of his face bore the remnants of a barely healed scar that stretched from his forehead down to his jawline, a constant reminder of battles fought and won.

His attire was simple: black combat boots, dark jeans, and a fitted jacket that concealed his most notable feature—a state-of-the-art prosthetic arm, made of sleek carbon fiber and equipped with deadly capabilities. The artificial limb gleamed in the moonlight.

As the soldier approached the entrance to Artemis' apartment, he knew that his moment had arrived. It was time for Artemis to pay the ultimate price for her boyfriend's cheek.

As the soldier's boots echoed against the pavement, he glanced back at the black Bentley parked discreetly down the street. The car's engine hummed softly, a low purr that spoke of luxury and power. Behind the wheel sat his butler, a small man with a silvering hairline who had served the soldier loyally for years.

Reginald was more than just a butler; he was a source of information, a confidant, as skilled in gathering intelligence as he was in preparing the soldier's favorite single malt.

Reginald was the one who'd found Artemis' address. He'd determined her airline ticket wasn't until the morning. She was attempting to flee the country...

He smiled.

So close, yet so far.

She'd nearly reached the finish line.

He pictured their faces, so strikingly different—Artemis, her coal-black hair framing delicate features, her eyes sharp with intelligence; and Forester, a mountain of a man with disheveled hair, his palm scarred like an old roadmap. The soldier reveled in the anticipation of what was to come, the thrill of the hunt coursing through his veins.

"Are you certain they're in there?" he whispered into a tiny earpiece, his voice laced with eagerness.

"It is where they sleep, sir," came Reginald's crisp reply. "Our source has confirmed their presence."

"Excellent," the soldier said, allowing himself a cold smile. "I hope they feel safe. Warm..." he trailed off, glancing at the second-floor window above.

"Understood, sir. I'll remain on standby should you require assistance."

"Thank you, Reginald. And prepare a toast for our imminent victory."

"Of course, sir. Your favorite single malt will be ready upon your return."

"Excellent." The soldier cut the connection and took a deep breath, steeling himself for the task ahead. As he stepped into the shadows of the apartment building, he whispered a vow into the night's chill air. Only he could hear the words.

The soldier paused before the entrance of the apartment building, his eyes glinting with cunning as he assessed the situation. He had left nothing to chance, using his immense wealth to ensure the building manager was handsomely compensated for his cooperation. Just as promised, the front door had been conveniently left unlocked, allowing him easy access.

"Money does have its advantages," he mused to himself as he tried the door handle. It turned effortlessly in his gloved hand, and a smirk tugged at the corner of his lips.

As he moved through the dimly lit hallway, the soldier's footsteps were silent, his movements fluid and precise like a panther stalking its prey. He had trained for years, honing his body into a lethal weapon capable of delivering swift and merciless vengeance to those who crossed him.

He ascended the stairs with stealthy grace, his prosthetic arm barely making a sound as it gripped the railing.

He spotted the apartment unit at the top of the stairs, and he approached it, his eyes zeroing in on the dark threshold.

He tried the handle.

Also unlocked. Click.

He pushed it in. The building manager had performed marvelously.

The door to the apartment swung open with a soft creak, revealing a living space that was unnervingly still. A solitary ray of moonlight pierced through the window blinds, casting eerie shadows across the floor.

His breath echoed in the cramped space, spreading before him like an echoing call.

But there was no answer—only the persistent ticking of a wall clock and the distant hum of the city outside.

He frowned, glancing around the space.

The furniture was untouched. There were dishes in the sink.

He smiled.

He moved down the hall towards the bedroom, approaching the door at the end of the hall.

He'd memorized the blueprints before the mission. he'd always had a good memory.

A long memory.

The soldier paused at the door, listening for any noises coming from the other side. He heard nothing but the sound of his own breathing, steady and controlled. A sense of anticipation and excitement coursed through him as he reached for the door-knob.

The door opened with a soft click, and the soldier stepped inside, his eyes adjusting to the darkness. He could make out the shape of a large bed in the center of the room, its covers rumpled and tossed to the side.

He moved closer to the bed, his heart racing with anticipation.

But as he drew closer, his eyes widened in shock and disbelief.

The bed was empty.

There was no one there.

He stood frozen in place, his mind racing as he tried to process what was happening. Had he been too late? Had they somehow managed to escape?

He heard a soft sound behind him and whirled around, his prosthetic arm poised to strike. But there was no one there. He was alone in the room.

He scowled out the window now, staring across the city beyond.

He pressed his earbud. "Why aren't they here," he said simply, his voice clear and precise, like the cleaned edge of a sharpened knife.

"Sir?" came the reply.

"They're not here."

"I... sir, their itinerary was for tomorrow."

"A dummy," he replied simply.

"Excuse me?"

"You're looking at the wrong ticket," he snapped. "Where is it headed to?"

"Guatemala, sir."

"Cameron isn't going to Guatemala."

"You're... you're certain sir?"

He scowled so deeply that he thought he might sprain something. "I know him, Reginald. He's not going to Guatemala. They duped you. They tricked you."

"I'm s-sorry sir."

"I don't care. You will punish yourself for this."

"Yes, sir. Anything else, sir?"

The soldier hung up, feeling his simmering rage bubbling now.

They were gone.

They'd left dishes in the sink. They'd left their things behind.

But they were gone.

The bed was rumpled, but the cabinet drawers were open. A few items of clothing were clearly missing judging by the dust imprints in the wood.

They were gone.

Forester had escaped!

Again.

His eyes flashed, and his temper flared.

Sometimes, he simply couldn't control his temper. It was like white hot heat, starting in his chest, and shooting in bursts of cortisol to the tips of his fingers.

He found himself breathing heavily now; rage burbling up.

And then he screamed.

It was a wild, undulating howl—like the ferocious call of a hungered wolf.

Before he even realized what he was doing, he flung the bed against the wall, ripping it from the ground.

The sound of the bed slamming into the wall echoed through the empty apartment, but the soldier barely registered it. His mind was consumed with fury.

He picked up a nearby chair and hurled it across the room, the wood splintering on impact. He let out another scream, the sound raw and primal as he unleashed his anger.

He slammed his fist into the window. Again. And again.

The glass shattered in a shower of sharp fragments, exploding outward into the night. A few shards clung to his skin, drawing thin trails of blood, but he didn't feel the pain. All he felt was the overwhelming rage, the need to destroy something, anything.

He turned back to the room, his eyes blazing with fury. He saw the remnants of the furniture, the scattered debris, the chaos he had wrought. And he felt a sense of satisfaction.

But it was a fleeting feeling.

As the adrenaline subsided, the soldier's mind began to clear. He realized the futility of his rage, the emptiness of his victory. He had lost again. Forester had escaped, and he was still out there, plotting and scheming. The soldier had won a battle, but he had lost the war.

He sank to the ground, his body trembling with exhaustion. He felt the cold air on his skin, the scent of shattered glass and broken wood.

He had always been a soldier, an instrument of death. And he enjoyed it. He took a deep breath, forcing himself to think clearly.

He couldn't let his emotions cloud his judgment.

He let out a long blast through his nostrils, taking in the room around him. And he realized something else.

In the midst of the man's destructive rampage, a soft knock echoed through the chaos. A timid voice followed, "Hello? Is everything all right in there?"

The soldier froze, his blood boiling at the interruption. He took another steadying breath, attempting to suppress his seething anger as he turned towards the door, and he stepped into the hall, peering towards where a woman stood in the open door of the apartment.

The neighbor, a frail elderly woman with gray hair and kind eyes peered into the apartment, her concern evident on her wrinkled face. "Oh dear," she murmured.

"Get out," the man snarled, clenching his prosthetic hand into a fist.

"Is there anything I can do to help?" she asked, ignoring his hostility. Her eyes locked onto his, radiating empathy. "Are you friends with the nice girl who lives here?"

"Friends?" he said, taking a step towards her.

She shrunk back as if sensing the rage radiating from him.

"Who are you?" she inquired gently, her curiosity outweighing her fear.

He growled, before lunging forward, grabbing her frail neck with his prosthetic arm.

It wasn't a complicated process.

It took very little time.

He relished the feeling of power that surged through him as her body went limp, extinguishing the light in her once-warm eyes.

He tossed her carcass aside, stepping over her broken form.

He resisted the urge to spit in disgust.

DNA evidence.

He'd have Reginald reclaim the glass pieces with his blood.

He marched out of the apartment now, his lungs shuddering with rapid, shallow puffs, his frown deep.

"Bring the car around," he snapped into his earpiece.

"Y-yes, sir," came the panicked voice. He imagined he heard pain in the sound as well. A punishment already carried out, perhaps?

A missing finger? Another scar?

He'd decide if it fit the crime of negligence.

The soldier marched away from the dead woman draped across the open doorway.

Forester had evaded him once more.

But he was the hunter.

He wouldn't stop until Cameron had suffered.

CHAPTER 1

As the private plane touched down on the equally exclusive runway, Artemis' coal-black hair stayed tucked behind her ears, her pretty features set in a determined expression.

She stared out the window at the city beyond, hoping that what lay ahead was better than what they'd all left behind.

She glanced at her family.

Her father, leaning back in one chair, a self-satisfied smirk on his features. Forester, arms crossed behind his head, was chewing a couple peanuts he'd taken from the tray of a sleeping man across the aisle.

And her sister, Helen. Helen was busy playing a chess match on the small, upright computer she'd brought with her.

Everyone was here...

Except Tommy.

Artemis frowned, sighing to herself as she remembered the family meeting only a couple nights before.

Everyone had been on board with the move. Everyone except Tommy, of course.

She frowned, crossing her arms, tucking her hands inside the sleeves of her second-hand, online-purchased sweater.

Her mismatched eyes studied the impressive city skyline, but she didn't focus. Her mind kept slipping back to the conversation with Tommy.

"Hell no!" he'd said. "I'm not moving across the damn world; this is home."

But it wasn't home anymore. Not after what happened. Not after the scandals that had rocked their family's reputation.

Her father's fake papers rested on the table in front of him.

Jasper Talisman.

She rolled her eyes at the chosen name—her father always did have a flair for the dramatic.

But money bought a lot, including discretion from private airfields.

The money she'd received for finding a billionaire's daughter was still weighing heavy on her, but it had opened up new options.

For all of them.

She had needed a fresh start. A chance to rebuild.

Forester was technically on-leave with the FBI.

She glanced at the tall man as he popped another peanut into his mouth. He spotted her looking and winked, nodding to the bathroom at the back of the plane and raising a quick, questioning eyebrow.

She tilted her head in slight confusion then realized what he was implying and blushed; her eyes quickly darted to Helen.

But her sister was too engrossed in her match to notice the proposition.

Forester just shrugged and leaned back again, still watching her with a pleased look on his face. There was an almost leonine quality to the way he lounged, a self-satisfied smirk on his face.

"Whachoo lookin' at, Checkers?" he said, still watching her.

She just shook her head, flashing a quick smile, and mouthed the word 'later'.

He grinned.

He was often grinning nowadays—especially when the two of them were together.

The self-proclaimed sociopath with a background as a professional cage fighter had always been cheeky, playful.

But it was only in recent months he'd seemed genuinely happy.

In a way, this made her glad.

In another way, it terrified her to her core.

A lot of his happiness, it had felt, seemed to be due to her. When she was around, he smiled. When she wasn't...

She didn't know what he did, but it was different; she knew that much.

The airplane came to a full stop now, and she saw the lights above her seat turn off, indicating it was safe to get up and prepare to disembark onto the runway.

A car would be waiting for them on the tarmac in the private airfield.

As she got to her feet, she couldn't help but look out the window again, studying the Istanbul skyline once more.

It was breathtaking, with its towering minarets and glittering lights. It was a city full of history and mystery, and she couldn't wait to explore it.

The limousine was waiting for them when they stepped out of the plane. The driver opened the door for them, and they all piled in.

Artemis sat in silence, watching as the city passed by outside. She couldn't shake the feeling that they were running away from their problems instead of facing them head-on. But this suited her just fine. She'd learned a long time ago that the best way to avoid a problem... was to avoid a problem.

Besides, it was too late to turn back now. They were committed to this new life, this new opportunity. Her father's fake identity had gotten him into the country, but the more they tested the border, the more dangerous it would be.

She glanced over at her older sister Helen, whose curly brown locks bounced gently with every jolt of the limousine.

"Welcome to Istanbul!" declared Otto from where he sat backward, facing his offspring, his blonde curls reminiscent of a much younger man. His eyes crinkled with excitement as he smiled at his daughters. "A new chapter awaits us, my darlings." He held onto Forester's scarred forearm, giving it a small pat in time with his words and jostling the tattered travel guide in the bigger man's hands.

Cameron glanced down, amused, and quirked an eyebrow at Artemis.

She just shrugged, half-heartedly suppressing a grin of her own.

Forester smiled back at Artemis. He then attempted to read aloud from the guidebook, mispronouncing the Turkish words, creating an amusingly butchered version of the language.

"Ah, yes," he chuckled, "the Ayşe Sofya... no, wait, it's Aya Sofya! And, uh, Kapalı Çarşı... or is it Kapalıçarşı?" He scratched his head, chuckling at his own mistakes. "This language is a bit t ricky, huh?"

Artemis laughed along with him, her spirits lifted by Forester's light-hearted approach to their new surroundings.

"Alright, let's try this one more time," Forester said, clearing his throat dramatically. "Welcome to Istanbul, the city where East meets West, and, well, where my pronunciation skills go south!"

Artemis allowed herself a small smile.

It was nice to find simple pleasure in amusing comments. Nice to not have to face death and decay at every step.

It was just... nice.

She allowed herself a quick nod of agreement with the direction of her own thoughts.

No murders. No crimes.

Just freedom.

And hopefully, it would continue that way.

Once their limousine deposited them on a street near the third bridge, the group stepped out of the vehicle into an engulfing cacophony of sounds and colors. Istanbul's vibrant energy pulsed through the air, as car horns blared and street vendors called out to potential customers. Artemis' senses were overwhelmed by the array of exotic scents wafting from nearby food stalls, each aroma more enticing than the last.

"Wow," Helen murmured, her eyes wide with wonder. "This place is alive."

Artemis nodded, feeling her pulse quicken in response to the city's relentless tempo. It was a far cry from the quiet, subdued life she had led up until now, but she welcomed the change, though, it did cause her to take a couple nervous steps closer to Cameron.

"Look over there," Otto said, pointing towards a distant skyline. "That's the Blue Mosque."

Artemis followed his gaze, her breath catching in her throat at the sight of the magnificent structure dominating the horizon. The mosque's grandeur was unparalleled, its domes and minarets reaching skyward with an elegance that made her heart ache. She couldn't help but feel a sense of awe and wonder as she took in the architectural marvel.

"Huh. I prefer Disney World," Forester remarked, his voice filled with indifference.

"Neanderthal," Artemis replied.

"Bourgois," he retorted.

"Do you know what that word even means?"

"Nope, but I like how it sounds."

She shook her head, pushing at his arm.

"Let's start by finding our accommodation," Otto suggested. "We can explore more of Istanbul later."

"Sounds like a plan," Forester said, retrieving his travel guide once more. With a determined nod, he began to navigate them through the chaos of the city streets, each step taking them further into the heart of their new home.

"Artemis, look!" Helen exclaimed, pointing to a swirling mass of pigeons that erupted from the cobblestone pathway as an old vendor tossed them seeds. Artemis' eyes widened in fascination as the birds took flight, their wings beating in unison like a rhythmic dance.

"Amazing," breathed Artemis, momentarily distracted from her thoughts of chess and victory. They continued to weave through the throngs of people, the clamor of voices echoing around them in a cacophony of languages and laughter.

"Ah, this is more like it," Otto said with a smile, his eyes crinkling as he took in the scene before them. They had entered a bustling market, where street vendors hawked their wares with practiced ease. The air was filled with the mouthwatering scents of exotic spices and freshly baked bread, mingling with the ever-present aroma of strong Turkish coffee.

"Forester, I hope you're paying attention to where we're going," warned Helen playfully, giving him a gentle nudge as they passed a stall laden with bright textiles. "We don't want to get lost now."

"Of course!" Forester replied, feigning indignation. He held up the travel guide triumphantly.

"Is that so?" Artemis asked, raising an eyebrow skeptically. As much as she appreciated Forester's enthusiasm, she couldn't help but doubt his navigational skills.

"See for yourself," Forester challenged, holding out the book for her inspection. Artemis glanced at the map, then back at the vibrant chaos surrounding them. She frowned, trying to make sense of the twisting streets and alleys.

"Maybe we should ask for directions," Otto suggested diplomatically, casting a sidelong glance at Forester. "Let's see if we can find someone who speaks English."

Suddenly, it was as if a challenge had been issued.

All three of the Blythes began studying the figures around them. Each one looking for an English speaker based on intuition, instinct, and physical cues.

The three of them had all prided themselves on their minds. Their father had once been a successful mentalist, and his daughters were both accomplished at reading body language and the like.

Artemis glanced at one man with a camera. Clearly a tourist, but no... too blond. German.

Her eyes moved along to another stall, spotting a woman with a child in tow. But the woman was moving quickly away, and the English graphic on her shirt disappeared in the crowd.

Forester seemed oblivious to this makeshift competition being held between the Blythes, and he contented himself with oohing and aahing over the market stall wares.

As they continued through the market, their path took them past a series of historic buildings, their ancient facades standing in stark contrast to the modern city that had grown up around them. Artemis felt a shiver of excitement at the thought of exploring these relics from the past, her keen mind already cataloging their stories and secrets.

"Look, there's the Bosphorus Bridge," Otto pointed out, as they emerged from the maze of narrow streets onto a wide waterfront promenade. The sun glinted off the water, casting a shimmering glow across the Bosphorus Strait.

"Wow," Helen breathed, her eyes widening with amazement. "It's beautiful."

"Indeed," agreed Artemis, her gaze locked on the magnificent structure. The bridge arched gracefully over the water, its steel cables forming a delicate web against the sky. She could just make out the distant silhouettes of boats navigating the strait, the churning wake of their passage rippling beneath the towering span.

"Quite an engineering feat," Forester noted, his voice filled with admiration.

"Incredible," Otto mused, watching the sunlight dance across the waves.

Helen tensed suddenly.

Artemis noticed it first; the way her sister went suddenly still, staring across the water towards the bridge. She watched her older sister closely, feeling a slow, creeping sense of anxiety.

Helen was the gentlest soul Artemis knew.

But she wasn't always this way.

Her mind was cruel to her, and Helen suffered at its whims sometimes.

She'd been on medicine to deal with the darker tendencies, and being around her family had also helped.

But one of the concerns Tommy had presented when they'd proposed the move had been Helen's condition.

What if she got worse?

Otto had suggested that fresh air, new sites, and the release of pressure from their family's history might do her some good.

They had already planned a trip to the Black Sea.

But now, Helen looked alarmed.

"Are you alright?" Artemis said quietly.

Her sister was staring off across the water, her eyes lingering on something under the bridge.

"What is it?" Artemis said, a bit more firmly.

Helen hesitated then pointed.

"Look," she whispered.

Artemis followed her sister's gaze, and then she froze.

Flashing lights were speeding towards the bridge. Bright, pulsing police lights. And the sirens could now just be heard, cast back their way from the Bosphorus as if reflected off the water.

Artemis and the others watched now, each of them poised, tense.

The Blythe family had a tenuous relationship with law enforcement at best.

Helen was a killer at large.

Their father was an innocent man convicted of her crimes.

And Forester...

He was along for the ride.

But Artemis was able to breath a bit easier as she realized the sirens were heading away from them.

"Wonder what that's all about," Otto said slowly, curiosity creeping into his voice.

"I don't," Cameron said, turning promptly. He shook his head. "Ignore it. None of our damn business—and, aha! Told you I was a genius."

"You didn't say that," Helen countered.

"Well, I'm telling you now. There's our new home!"

He pointed towards a sign on the outside of a black, metal gate that simply read Paradise City.

Artemis stared at the gated community. She hadn't known what to expect in Istanbul, but the black gate circling the, apparently, new construction provided a semblance of protection... solitude, perhaps.

She approached the site with the others, moving quickly through the cultured streets and toward their new home.

She tried not to glance towards the sirens again.

But more had joined the first batch. She spotted nearly ten police cars zooming in the same direction.

Ignore it, she scolded herself. Just ignore it.

She forced a smile as the security guard in the white booth by the black fence grinned at them. "Merhaba," he said, "Nasilsiniz, arkadashlar?"

Forester consulted his handbook. "Saul. No. Sol. No... hang on. Banyo?"

The guard smirked. "English?"

"Yes, please," Helen said. And then she replied, in nearly perfect Turkish, "Biz Istanbulu fazla bilmiyoruz. Cok ozurdilerim."

The guard beamed.

Forester glanced over, quirking an eyebrow.

He leaned into Artemis as Helen and the guard exchanged information, and the gate began to open.

"Your sister knows Turkish?"

"Now she does," Artemis replied. "Before the plane ride, she didn't."

Forester blinked in surprise. People who hadn't grown up with Helen, well, they usually didn't understand her computer-like mind.

But for Artemis, it was par for the course.

She smiled as her sister gained them entry into their new community, and she followed through the opening black gates.

And yet somehow, she couldn't help but think of the sirens in the distance and wonder what horrors they heralded.

Chapter 2

Settling in their new digs had taken nearly two hours. Finding the nearest chess club, however, had only taken five minutes.

In part, this was because Artemis had chosen this gated site specifically for its chess club.

And now, Artemis and her sister faced each other over the checkered board, sitting on the patio outside the club. Through the windows, one could see figures of all ages engrossed in mind games, set out on long, rectangular tables with roll-up boards between them.

The faint tick-tick-tick of chess clocks was only interrupted by the tap of a finger clicking the clock button.

Occasionally, the Turkish players would say something like "Shah or Shah-mat," which Artemis didn't understand yet, but knew her sister did.

The sun crawled westward, casting a warm golden glow over the chessboard that stood between Artemis and Helen. The sisters sat opposite each other in silent contemplation, their eyes locked in fierce competition as they meticulously plotted their next moves. The wind whispered through the trees, rustling their leaves like quiet applause.

"Your move," Helen said gently, her curly brown hair dancing in the breeze. Despite her kind nature, she was a formidable opponent. She'd taught her younger sister, after all.

Artemis studied the board, her mismatched eyes observing every piece and its potential path. She considered her options, weighing the pros and cons of each move. Her sister's knight threatened her queen, but if she moved her bishop to intercept, she would leave her king vulnerable. Artemis tapped her fingers lightly on the table, her mind racing through the various possibilities and outcomes. She was an analytical machine, calculating risk and reward in mere moments.

"Check," she announced with a sly grin, sliding her rook across the board to a strategic position. She glanced up at Helen, who furrowed her brow in concentration. Artemis knew she had placed her sister in a difficult situation; it would take a clever maneuver to escape the trap she'd set.

"Interesting," Helen replied, her voice barely above a whisper. She stared at the board, her eyes darting back and forth. Artemis watched her with a mixture of admiration and anticipation. She loved these games; not just for the challenge they presented, but for the bond they forged between her and her sister.

"Bishop to e5," Helen declared, moving her piece out of harm's way while simultaneously defending her king. She looked up at Artemis.

"Very well played," Artemis conceded, her mind already working through the implications of Helen's move. She knew she couldn't rely on simple tricks; she needed to outthink her opponent, to see several moves ahead and anticipate Helen's strategy. The game was a mental battlefield, and Artemis thrived in its chaos.

The shadows grew longer as the sun dipped lower, casting an eerie glow on the patio where Artemis and Helen played their match. The scent of freshly cut grass mingled with the faint aroma of a distant cooking fire—mangal, Helen had called it—marking the approach of autumn. Leaves rustled underfoot as pedestrians strolled by, circling the walking paths that cut through the gated community.

"Knight to f3," Artemis murmured, moving her piece decisively.

"Rook to d8."

"Ah, you two play quite brilliantly," a voice interrupted, shattering the veil of concentration that had enveloped the sisters. They looked up to find a middle-aged man with graying hair and a bushy mustache standing nearby, his eyes alight with admiration. He fumbled for a moment with his words, speaking in a language Artemis didn't understand, though she did catch the apology of, "Ozur dilerim." But then he switched seamlessly to flawless English. "My apologies, I did not mean to intrude."

Artemis shifted in her seat, unused to such praise from a stranger. She exchanged a glance with Helen, who seemed equally surprised but pleased by the man's comments.

"You have played long?" he said.

Helen hesitated, then pointed at her sister. "She has."

"You have too," Artemis replied quickly.

"I'm not a professional, though." "You are?" the man said, his dark eyes widening. "A professional player?" Artemis shifted uncomfortably. She gave a quick shrug and a half nod.

The man's eyes widened even further. "Truly, a professional! And so young!" he exclaimed, his voice filled with admiration. "I am a coach, but not much experienced in competition. Do you compete in tournaments?"

Artemis hesitated for a moment, then nodded. "Yes, I do," she said, her voice laced with a hint of embarrassment.

The man smiled widely, his mustache twitching with pleasure. "Wonderful! Absolutely wonderful! I myself am an avid chess player, you see. I come here every evening to play with my friends."

He gestured to the club behind him.

"I have never seen such skill in someone so young," the man continued, his eyes sparkling with excitement. "Would you be interested in a game with me? I would be honored to play against a professional."

Artemis hesitated for a moment, a flicker of doubt crossing her mind. The man's enthusiasm made her wonder if he was a more skilled player than he let on. But then she thought of the thrill of the game, the rush of adrenaline as she plotted her strategy and made her moves.

"Sure," she said, with a smile. "I would love to play."

The man beamed with pleasure, his eyes twinkling with excitement. "Wonderful! Truly wonderful! Let us begin, then."

He pulled up a chair and began setting up the pieces, his hands moving with a grace born of years of practice.

Artemis winced as she realized he'd meant now.

Helen didn't mind having her pieces moved, though. She stood up carefully, and stepped back, allowing the man access to the seating.

"I... sorry," Artemis said suddenly. "Would you mind if we finished our game first?"

The man paused, stared at Helen, then Artemis, and then held a hand over his mouth.

"Oh my... Oh... oh my. I'm so sorry. What an aptal erif I've been. I didn't..." he shook his head, stepping back hurriedly and nearly stumbling over the chair.

"It's fine," Helen said softly. Then, from memory, she set the board up in the position it had been before he'd accidentally disturbed it.

"I... I will have to play with my friend—he is waiting. But... just..." he hesitated, shrugging once.

"Would you," the man paused again, clearly weighing his words carefully, "entertain the idea of sharing your expertise with the younger kids in our chess club? They could learn a great deal from players like yourselves."

Artemis' brow furrowed as she considered the proposition. Teaching others was a responsibility she hadn't anticipated, and it stirred a mix of emotions within her.

"Of course!" Helen's voice was bright and animated, her eyes reflecting the same eagerness as she turned to the chess coach. "We'd be more than happy to help the children learn. When would you like?"

The corners of Artemis' lips twitched in a half-smile, appreciating her sister's generosity, but she couldn't shake the nagging doubts that gnawed at her mind. Sometimes it was hard to forget what Helen had done. What Helen had been.

But no.

Not Helen. Something else.

Artemis kept reminding herself of this truth, though it was an easy one to forget.

"Is something the matter?" the coach asked, his perceptive gaze falling on Artemis.

She hesitated, her fingers unconsciously tapping a rhythm on the edge of the chessboard as she weighed the implications of teaching.

"Please," the coach said, his voice gentle yet persuasive. "I understand your reservations, but I assure you, your assistance would be invaluable to our club."

He didn't understand at all. But it wasn't his fault.

How many people had a serial killer for a sister?

But they'd come here for a fresh start.

Helen deserved it. After everything she'd been through.

Artemis exhaled slowly, her eyes darting from her sister's encouraging smile to the expectant expression of the coach. With a nod, she finally acquiesced. "Alright, we'll do it."

"Excellent!" The chess player beamed, clapping his hands together in delight.

As Artemis listened to more expressions of gratitude from the man, her gaze was drawn to a figure not far off.

She spotted them through the glass windows and watched where the person was hunched over a desk in the back of the club, through an open office door.

It was difficult to discern at first, but as she focused, it became clearer—the person's shoulders were shaking. Were they crying?

Artemis frowned, staring through the glass. The door was slightly ajar, revealing just a sliver of the dimly lit room within.

"Excuse me," Artemis interrupted, her curiosity piqued, as she looked toward the source of the sight. "I couldn't help but notice there seems to be someone upset in the back office. Is everything alright?" Her voice was hesitant, but her eyes conveyed genuine concern.

The chess coach's jovial demeanor faltered for a moment, replaced by an expression of worry. He hesitated, glancing briefly at the door, then back at Artemis. "Ah, yes," he said, his tone subdued. "It's been... a difficult time for some of our members lately. Please don't concern yourself with it."

Despite the reassurances, she considered pushing further, seeking more information about the situation. But she also knew that the coach had been gracious enough to welcome her and Helen into the club, so prying might not be the most tactful approach.

"Of course," she replied, forcing a small smile, even though her thoughts raced with questions. Who was the person crying? What could have happened to cause such distress?

She thought of the sirens near the bridge and felt a cold shiver.

The man mistook her expression, though, and paused.

"It... it isn't a big deal. She... my daughter is having a difficult time. It's been tough for her lately." He rubbed his forehead, a quiet sigh escaping him.

"Is everything all right?" Artemis asked, trying to gauge whether she should push further or offer some sort of comfort. Her heart ached at the sight of the grieving girl, but she knew better than to interject herself into a stranger's pain without invitation.

The coach hesitated for a moment, seemingly weighing his options. "Her best friend passed away recently," he finally admitted, his voice barely above a whisper. "They were both members of this chess club—talented young players with so much potential. It's been hard on all of us. Quite... shocking. Yes, that's the word. Shocking."

"When did this happen?" Helen said.

"Just this morning," he replied. "Her friend was found dead. It was really bad. Very, very bad," he said.

The more agitated he became, the more gaps Artemis noticed in his English.

But he calmed slowly, shaking his head sadly, and said, "It is a big pity. She deserved better."

"What was her name?"

"Irem Korkmaz," he said.

"Korkmaz," replied Helen. "it means fearless?"

"Yes," he replied, smiling. "You know this?"

"I've picked up a little."

"She died this morning?" Artemis said. She felt a chill run down her spine.

"It's... don't concern yourself," he said quickly. "Two pretty ladies like you? It isn't worth listening to such horrible things."

"How horrible?" Helen asked, concern in her eyes.

The man glanced through the window once more at his weeping daughter.

He swallowed, staring.

And for a brief moment, Artemis caught the pain hidden behind his eyes as well.

A pain that was clearly masked. Perhaps it was a cultural thing; did men in Turkey think it was okay to cry?

Even as she had the thought, she suppressed it.

She felt out of her depth once more. A stranger in a strange land.

And yet... the man was so genuinely friendly. So kind.

And now she could see the empathy in the pained expression.

She felt her heart go out to him.

But he was shaking his head, and said, after a bit, "She was drowned. If you really must know. Murdered."

Chapter 3

THE MOON CAST A silvery glow through the large windows of the chess club, its beams illuminating the dark room. Artemis, her coal black hair falling past her shoulders, sat in contemplative silence, her pretty features devoid of makeup and her attire simple yet elegant. She was the only one left at the club, her dedication to the game evident as she meticulously moved the pieces on the board.

Even Helen had retired for the evening after instructing a couple of younger girls on the finer points of the Sicilian Defense. Their father had wanted a backgammon partner, accusing Forester of cheating, so Helen had obliged.

But Artemis didn't mind.

She found the quiet, the isolation somewhat peaceful.

As the quiet night wore on, the chess club seemed almost suspended in time. The soft hum of the air conditioning provided a soothing backdrop to the rhythmic sound of chess pieces being placed on the board. Rows of empty tables and chairs lined the room, while framed pictures of past champions adorned the walls, their eyes seeming to follow Artemis's every move.

Artemis's fingers danced across the chessboard, deftly maneuvering the pieces as if they were an extension of her own thoughts. Her eyes darted between the squares, calculating each move with intense focus. It was in this solitude that she found peace, away from the noise and distractions of the world outside. The gentle clink of the pieces against the board echoed through the otherwise silent club, a testament to the hours she had invested in mastering the art of chess.

The hush of the room lulled Artemis into a tranquil state of mind, allowing her to fully immerse herself in the complexities of the game. Despite the late hour, her mental acuity remained sharp, honed by years of practice and countless matches played both against worthy opponents and within the confines of her own mind. This was where she felt most alive, her intellect challenged and rewarded in equal measure by the endless possibilities that lay before her on the chessboard.

As the clock on the wall ticked softly in the background, Artemis's fingers glided over the chess pieces, her keen eyes darting across the board, anticipating the next move. She was reliving one of her favorite historical matches—the legendary encounter between Anatoly Karpov and Garry Kasparov in 1985—a contest that had enthralled the world and demonstrated the highest level of strategic mastery. In her mind, she was part of that grand battle, pitting her wits against the titans of the game.

As her queen captured another piece, a faint creak resonated through the room. Artemis's head snapped up, surprise registering on her face. A young woman stood hesitantly at the entrance of the club, her tear-stained cheeks glistening under the dim lights. Her eyes were red-rimmed and swollen, betraying the depth of her anguish.

It was the same woman Artemis had seen bent over in the back office.

The coach's daughter.

She stared at the young, Turkish woman. More a girl, really. Not much older than seventeen.

She had large, brown eyes set in a face that was both delicate and striking. Her hair was a mass of tangled curls, as if she had been running her hands through it in distress. There was something about her that drew Artemis's attention.

"Are you alright?" Artemis asked softly, rising from her chair.

The girl shook her head, her eyes brimming with tears. "No," she said, in slightly accented English, "I... sorry. I didn't know anyone was still here."

"Do you come here often?" Artemis said.

"My father runs the place."

"Oh. I don't think he's here."

"No," the girl said quickly. "That's not what I meant. I just... I come here when I want to get away sometimes." She shrugged sheepishly as if embarrassed.

Artemis nodded, understanding the need for solitude all too well. "I know what you mean. This place is like a sanctuary."

The girl sniffled, wiping her nose on the sleeve of her hoodie. "I'm sorry. I didn't mean to intrude."

The young woman hesitated, clearly struggling to find her words. "I... I saw you play once," she said finally, desperation seeping into her tone. "You're Artemis Blythe, aren't you?"

Artemis's guard went up, her thoughts churning with a whirlwind of questions and doubts. "Yes, I am," she said warily, her hand tightening around a captured chess piece.

45

"You were in the blitz game a few days ago. I saw you win."

"You watch online chess?"

"Here, let me show you," the young woman said, pulling out her phone. For a moment, she seemed distracted from her tears. Her fingers trembled as she tapped on the screen and then handed it to Artemis. Artemis' mismatched eyes narrowed as she studied the image: a screenshot of the online broadcast from her recent blitz tournament.

"Your skills are incredible," the young woman continued, her voice cracking with emotion. "You have such an amazing mind; I've never seen anyone play like you."

Artemis looked up from the phone, her expression softening just slightly at the unexpected praise. She handed the phone back, curiosity piqued. "Thank you," she said, her tone guarded but genuine.

She studied the young woman then asked, "What's your name?"

"Izel."

"Hello, Izel." Artemis paused, then in a gentle tone, she said, "You came here to speak with me, didn't you?"

Izel hesitated, looking suddenly alarmed. She cleared her throat and stammered, "I-I... I wouldn't say..." she trailed off, wincing, then sighed. "Yes."

"May I ask why?"

The young woman took a deep, shuddering breath, trying to compose herself. "My best friend," she began, tears welling up in her eyes once more. "Irem Korkmaz. She... she was murdered."

A heavy silence settled over the room, broken only by the young woman's choked sobs. Artemis felt a wave of sympathy wash over her, mixed with dread and uncertainty. She knew she should remain detached, uninvolved. And yet...

"What... I'm so sorry. But what does that have to do with me?"

The young woman looked surprised. "Because," she said, "you solve murders."

"Oh?"

Artemis felt a cold prickle move down her spine. She realized now, too late, that she never should've come to a chess club. The internet had a broad reach, and people here knew her from her blitz performances. So much for keeping a low profile.

"I... I didn't tell anyone who you were!" Izel said suddenly as if reading Artemis' reservations.

This was clearly an intelligent young woman. "But... I have no one else to go to." She shrugged. "The police won't listen."

Get up. Leave. The voice in her head kept issuing commands, but Artemis couldn't just abandon the girl, could she? Artemis thought of Helen.

"Please tell me more," Artemis whispered, locking eyes with the stranger's coal-black pupils, shimmering with tears of grief.

"The police, they're not listening," she said, a tremor in her voice. "They think they've found the murderer, but I know they haven't. They're just grasping at straws, trying to close the case quickly. It's not right."

Artemis studied the young woman's face, seeing the raw pain etched there.

"From what I've heard, they have two people in custody," the young woman continued, her voice wavering. "But it makes no sense. Neither of them had any reason to hurt Irem."

"Who do they have in custody?"

"I... I don't know their names."

"So how do you know..." Artemis paused, catching herself. She bit her lip as if to hold back the flood of words.

It wasn't any of her business, was it?

She didn't need to pry... but again, it was like she was sitting across from another type of chess puzzle, and this time, her curiosity was piqued.

"What makes you so sure they have the wrong person," Artemis said, "If you don't even know who they have."

"Because!" Izel exclaimed, "they think it was an honor killing. That's what I heard from my father."

"An honor killing?"

"Y-yes... Irem's family is from a traditional background. But Irem was different. She was a free spirit. She didn't follow the rules. She was in love with someone her family didn't approve of. And the police think they killed her for it."

The young woman's voice broke on the last word.

"I see," Artemis said slowly, her mind working to process the information. "But you don't believe it? And you think the two people they're questioning are family members of Irem's?"

"Yes!" Izel nodded. "Irem's family was traditional but they were good people. They loved her. The police are looking in the wrong place!"

"Please... you have to help me." The young woman's eyes, red and swollen from crying, pleaded with Artemis as she clutched her hands tightly in front of her chest. "Please," she implored, her voice cracking under the weight of her desperation. "My friend deserves better than this. Irem's family deserves to know the truth. I know you can help."

Artemis hesitated, feeling a surge of empathy for the young woman in front of her. She could see the raw pain etched into every line of her face, the deep sense of injustice that drove her to seek help in such an unlikely place. Artemis knew all too well the anguish of losing someone close, and she understood the powerful urge to uncover the truth, no matter the cost. Yet she couldn't shake the lingering doubts that clouded her mind, the nagging fear that getting involved in this case would only drag her back into a darkness she had tried so hard to leave behind.

"Listen," Artemis began, her voice soft but firm. "I understand what you're going through, and I want to help. But I need you to understand that this won't be like anything I've ever done before. I'll have to proceed carefully, discreetly. The last thing we want is to draw any unwanted attention."

The young woman nodded fervently, fresh tears streaming down her cheeks. "I know! I just want justice for Irem!"

A tense silence filled the room as Artemis studied the chessboard before her for a moment, the tension in the air palpable. Like a Grandmaster contemplating her next move, she weighed the risks and rewards of each potential course of action, knowing that a single misstep could lead to catastrophic consequences.

"Alright," she finally whispered, her eyes betraying a sort of resignation. "I'll look into it. I can't promise anything, but I'll do my best to find out what really happened to your friend."

CHAPTER 4

"YOU PROMISED HER WHAT?" Artemis' father demanded, gaping at his daughter where he leaned against a balcony railing.

In one hand he held a cigar, which trailed smoke up towards the night sky.

He smelled of whiskey, but his eyes were still attentive and alert.

Artemis was busy peering through the binoculars that Forester had happily procured.

Her brow wrinkled and she frowned as she looked towards the bridge, studying the police vehicles that were still blockading the harbor.

"So many cops for one girl," Artemis said softly.

She watched through the binoculars as three police officers seemed to be involved in a heated argument.

One of the men got physical with another, and the third officer stepped in between, trying to separate the first's grasping hands from the other's collar.

Behind them, a ferry boat sat on the water, tied off to the shore via a mooring post covered in black mussels. Artemis frowned at the scene through the binoculars, trying to make sense of it all.

"What do you see?" her father asked. "It's hard to tell," she said slowly. "Tempers are high."

"Anything else?"

"Not much," she replied.

He snorted, blowing cigar smoke from his nostrils. "You're slipping, Art. That's not how I taught you?"

She sighed, lowering her binoculars. "You want to take a shot?"

Her father shrugged, snatched the binoculars from her, and lifted the fringe of his curled, golden hair with the lenses as he affixed them to his eyes and studied the distant crime scene by the bridge.

"Well," he said, "For one... these things are smudged."

"They came like that."

"Your boyfriend's greasy paws seem to like roaming everywhere," her father said, coldly.

"And what is that supposed to mean? Actually—you know what—I don't want to know."

Her father lowered the binoculars in disgust, shrugged his shoulders, and said, "Only one way to do this properly." He snuffed out his cigar in an ashtray and moved towards the fire escape that led down from the balcony.

"Hey!" she protested, calling after her father as he moved under the moonlight, down the metal stairs, his footsteps somehow not clanging on the metal—he always had been light-footed.

She hastened after him, trying to call him back, but her father ignored her.

He seemed amused by her concern, but also, he was massaging the tip of his chin as he so often did when his curiosity was piqued.

She realized her father had been cooped up in a prison for years, then for weeks he'd been cooped up by Tommy, kept out of sight to avoid apprehension.

Now, though, he clearly wanted to stretch his legs.

Another country, another lease on life.

But it didn't do anything except tax Artemis' nerves. Her escaped-convict father was marching steadily toward police officers.

At the base of the fire escape, she managed to catch up with her old man as he walked with surefooted steps in the direction of the gathered law enforcement officers.

He moved quickly for a man twice her age, and she struggled to keep up.

The cool evening breeze lifted Artemis' coal-black hair as she peered over her father's shoulder, the Bosphorus Bridge looming in the distance. The iconic landmark cast a shadow on the dock ahead, silhouetting the Istanbul skyline.

"Dad, we shouldn't be here," Artemis said, her words urgent and hushed as they drew nearer. "This is a crime scene."

Her father slowed to a stroll, allowing her to catch up. Otto simply smiled, his eyes crinkling at the corners. He had a knack for getting into places he wasn't meant to be.

"Relax, Artemis," he replied, patting her arm reassuringly. "We're just taking a look."

As they approached the crime scene tape, Otto's focus strayed to a group of frustrated police officers arguing nearby. Their faces were flushed, their gestures animated.

Artemis couldn't understand the words they spoke, but her father—who had a similar polyglot affinity for language to Helen—leaned in, standing behind a stack of old, wooden crates. His brow furrowed, and he leaned closer to Artemis, whispering, "It seems the coroner is delayed. They're probably having a hard time finding someone willing to examine a body on such short notice."

Otto's eyes scanned the area, seeking an opportunity to make their move. Noticing a stack of crates nearby, he smirked and turned to Artemis. "Watch this."

With calculated precision, he pushed the top crate, sending it crashing to the ground. The resulting noise echoed across the dock, drawing the attention of the frustrated officers.

"Quickly, now!" Otto whispered urgently to Artemis, who hesitated for a split second before realizing if she stayed put, she'd be spotted.

Her father was pointing to a small gap between a shipping container and a concrete structure. The makeshift alley led towards the boat.

She cursed but realized she couldn't stay put and hastened after her father. As the cops went to investigate the noise, Artemis and Otto slipped down the dark alley, which led to the Turkish ferry boat.

"This is insane," Artemis hissed as they moved up a gangplank onto the boat. Her feet struck the metal with a faint clang. Every creak of the boat felt like a shout, announcing their presence.

"Isn't it thrilling?" Otto grinned, his excitement palpable. "If the coroner isn't here, dear," he said quietly, "that means the body still is."

He looked at her; she stared back.

For a moment, the two of them paused by the railing.

"You're joking," she whispered.

"Rarely."

She shot a look towards where the cops' backs were turned as they examined the smashed crates. The air of suspicion was all too apparent.

"You're the one who said we'd help Izel," her father pointed out. "This is us helping. Now move quietly, dear. You sound like a stampede of elephants."

He set off again before she could reply.

Grudgingly, and grumbling, she followed after him.

As they made their way through the vessel, Artemis couldn't help but notice the aging beauty of the ferry boat. The once vibrant colors had faded with time, a testament to the many journeys it had undertaken. She imagined the countless passengers who had walked these very halls, each with a unique story of their own.

"Here," Otto said, pointing to a line of caution tape that indicated the direction of the crime scene area. "This way."

They followed the tape, winding through the narrow corridors, the scent of saltwater and diesel fuel permeating the air. Artemis's heart raced with every step, her mind torn between fascination and apprehension.

The smell hit them first—an acrid, metallic odor that hung heavy in the air. Artemis wrinkled her nose, her eyes watering from the assault on her senses. As they rounded a corner, she saw it: the crime scene.

"Artemis, brace yourself," Otto warned, his voice barely audible.

Before them lay the lifeless body of Irem Korkmaz, shrouded half beneath a damp tarp. The dim lighting cast eerie shadows across the victim's face, and Artemis felt a chill snake its way up her spine. She swallowed hard, trying to quell the rising nausea as her father approached the body, his movements precise and methodical.

"Look at the water pooled around her," Otto said, gesturing to the dark puddle surrounding the corpse. "She was drowned—likely elsewhere—and brought here."

"Her hair is still wet," Artemis observed, her voice wavering. "Her skin... It's so pale."

"Indeed. Her lips have a faint blue tinge, another sign of asphyxiation due to drowning." Otto examined Irem's hands, lifting one gently with gloved fingers. "See these tiny bruises along her fingers? They suggest she struggled, tried to free herself from whatever—or whoever—held her under."

Artemis shivered, picturing the woman's desperate fight for survival. The very thought made her stomach churn, but she forced herself to focus on the task at hand.

"What about her clothes?" she asked, noting that Irem's attire appeared undisturbed. "Surely there would be some signs of a struggle if she was attacked?"

"An excellent point, my dear," Otto replied, studying the clothing more closely. "But perhaps her assailant incapacitated her before attempting to drown her. Or maybe she was lured into the water willingly, only to find herself trapped?"

Artemis frowned, the possibilities swirling in her mind like a maelstrom. As much as she wanted to solve this case and bring Irem's killer to justice, part of her wished they had never stumbled into this grisly scene.

"Come now, Artemis," Otto urged gently, his eyes meeting hers for a moment. "There is more to uncover here, and we mustn't let our emotions cloud our judgment."

Artemis knelt down beside a severed rope, her fingers gently exploring the frayed ends. She hesitated for a moment before examining Irem's ankle—her father had always taught her to respect the dead, but the pursuit of justice demanded that she set aside her personal feelings.

"Father, look at this," Artemis said, her voice barely above a whisper. "There are fibers and markings on her ankle."

"Hmm... She was tied." "And drowned..."

"Yes," Otto said, frowning. "If I had to guess, it seems like she was dragged behind the boat. See the way the rope is angled upwards?"

Artemis shivered, trying not to think what the young woman must've experienced in her last moments of life.

She had plain features, and her face was bloated now.

Artemis' dark eyes, narrowed with concentration, scanned the disarray of the crime scene. The damp air weighed heavily on her as she and Otto moved further apart, their steps whispering on the slick wooden deck. With each subtle creak, she imagined the boat groaning under the weight of its sorrowful secrets.

"Keep your eyes peeled for anything out of the ordinary," Otto whispered, his voice barely audible over the distant murmurings of the frustrated police officers. He bent down to examine a tangle of ropes, his fingers tracing the frayed ends like a spider weaving its web.

"Of course," Artemis murmured, her words a silent prayer for guidance. As she sifted through the debris, her thoughts wandered to the absence of a purse. Surely, Irem would have had one—she was a young, Turkish woman after all, and her pockets wouldn't have allowed for a wallet or keys.

"No purse," she said quietly.

Otto paused across the room, frowning. "Taken?" he asked.

"Other personal effects are there," Artemis said, pointing to a pair of sunglasses and a locket on the table by the body. "So why no purse?"

Her father frowned now, tapping his foot against the wooden flooring. "Huh," he said. He kicked aside the tangle of rope, looking under it.

Artemis moved to the desk, peering behind it, then checked under it.

No sign of a purse.

She frowned.

"Maybe it was lost when she was dragged behind the boat," Artemis said softly.

"Possibly. Likely, in fact."

Her father paused. "How come her personal effects aren't wet, though?" He pointed to the items on the desk.

The two of them approached, peering down at the sunglasses and the locket.

"Maybe they were dried?"

Her father then pointed to a hair scrunchie. "Dry as dust."

"Now that is peculiar," she said. "Do you think the killer removed her personal effects before killing her?"

"What for?"

"I don't know."

"You think he has her purse?"

"I think someone does."

Her father frowned. "Maybe she lost her purse when she was attacked."

"Or maybe someone stole it."

Her father nodded, his blue eyes flashing. He ran a hand daintily through his perfectly coifed hair. "I see... Well... Her phone isn't here."

Artemis paused and then snapped her fingers. "Good call," she said. "If the phone is in the purse, maybe we can track it."

"As long as the phone wasn't ruined by water, and as long as the purse isn't at the bottom of the Bosphorus," her father pointed out. Then he held up a finger, "And as long as that handsy boyfriend of yours is able to track the damn thing."

Artemis ignored this comment about Forester's hands. In fact, she was quite fond of Cameron, hands and all.

She was about to say something when the sound of footsteps caught her attention.

She stiffened. It sounded as if someone was on the boat. The coroner?

"Shit," she whispered. "Let's go. Now!"

Her father was still scanning the crime scene, so she caught his arm and hurried towards a sign marked Exit which would deposit them on the opposite side of the dock.

As they hurried away, Artemis hoped that it would be as simple as tracking a phone, caught in a stolen purse... If so, they'd have the killer in custody before morning.

And if not...

She frowned, glancing back at the body under the tarp.

Who killed someone like that?

Dragging their defenseless body along the water?

She shivered, shook her head, and picked up the pace, taking metal stairs two at a time alongside her father.

CHAPTER 5

THE DEAD OF NIGHT in Istanbul felt like a living, breathing thing. The darkness seemed to take on a life of its own, wrapping itself around the city's ancient structures and winding streets, swallowing up the faint glow of the moon. From Artemis' perspective, the shadows seemed to dance and shift like restless spirits, whispering secrets she could never quite grasp. There was a palpable sense of mystery that hung in the air.

And it was a mystery that saw Artemis and Cameron out late, both hunched over the glowing screen in Forester's calloused fighter's hands.

"Any luck?" Artemis asked, her voice barely above a whisper as they moved through the narrow, dimly lit streets of crowded, hastily-built apartments. Her father had told her about the *gecekondu* city, and from what she'd gathered, the term seemed to refer to the low-cost, improvised neighborhoods that popped up almost as if they'd sprung out of the ground overnight.

"Almost there," Forester replied, his eyes locked on the screen of the device in his hand. He was following the signal from the phone of the murder victim, Irem Korkmaz, and despite the odds, he seemed confident they would find something worthwhile.

"Left down this alley," Forester directed, and Artemis followed closely behind him, her coal-black hair swaying slightly as she moved.

As they continued to traverse the labyrinthine streets, Artemis pondered the gecekondu. The buildings, if they could be called that, were made of cardboard, stolen sheet metal, and poster board. The structures couldn't have been much sturdier than most carnival tents—but unlike carnival tents, the sights and smells of this place weren't the sort one paid a gate fee to access.

Rather, the whole place, under the Istanbul night sky, stretched out like a dark bruise on the outskirts of the city. The many overnight buildings were like scabs on top of the bruise, each one housing people who had nowhere else to go.

Artemis shivered, pulling her jacket tighter around her slender frame. This was not a place for the faint of heart, and she couldn't help but feel a sense of foreboding.

The brutal murder of Irem Korkmaz was a single thread, but the way she'd died... it all seemed strange.

She shivered, picturing Izel's pleading gaze as the young woman had begged Artemis to help with this case.

Had she made a mistake agreeing to help?

Only time would tell.

The gecekondu city stretched before them like a patchwork quilt, a cacophony of colors and textures that seemed to defy both logic and gravity. Makeshift structures clung precariously to one another, their cardboard walls and tin roofs barely protecting the residents from the elements. Artemis tried to imagine what it must be like to live in such a place—to call this precarious collection of debris and hope home.

"Forester, are you sure we're going the right way?" she asked, her voice laced with doubt as they navigated the narrow alleyways. She kept glancing at the phone in his hand. "Told you, GPS works here just the same as home. Besides, my BKA contact wouldn't lie." He shrugged.

"Why not?" she asked suspiciously.

"Hmm?"

"This BKA agent—German, right? Female?"

"Huh?"

"You heard me."

"I think we're getting closer," he said, clearly ignoring the question on purpose.

As they continued through the slum, Artemis couldn't help but notice the small details that made each makeshift dwelling unique—a faded photograph taped to a wall, a child's drawing scrawled on cardboard, a patchwork quilt draped over a rickety chair. Each was a testament to the resilience and creativity of the inhabitants, proof that even in the most desperate circumstances, people found ways to make a life for themselves.

"Ah, now we're talking," Cameron muttered to himself all of a sudden.

"What?"

"The GPS signal. I see it now."

She stared at the side of his head. "Hang on... you see it now."

Her hands clenched at her side so tightly that she felt her nails digging into her skin.

"What do you mean?"

He quirked an eyebrow at her. "Which word should I define?"

"Cameron! What have we been tracking if you haven't seen the GPS signal until now?"

"Oh, it's been there, just spotty. Coming and going. No biggie, Art. Hang on... lost it again." He wiggled his phone, tapping it with the flat of his other, scarred hand.

"Cameron!" she snapped.

"Goody!" he declared. "And we're back!"

Forester's long strides left Artemis almost jogging to keep up. The slum seemed to morph around them, the shadows of the cardboard shanties blending together in the dim light. Her breaths came in short, sharp bursts as her eyes darted from one dark corner to another, searching for any hint of danger.

"Slow down," she hissed, reaching out to grab Forester's arm. "You're going to get us both killed if we barrel through here like this."

"Relax," he replied, his voice low and steady. "I've got a good feeling about this place. Trust me."

She remembered how Cameron often said he was from the 'streets.' Whatever that meant. She'd mostly thought he was teasing, but she knew that the gym he helped out at often aided young men who didn't have any other options.

In a way, in a place like this, Cameron Forester almost felt at home.

They rounded a corner and stumbled upon a scene that, for a moment, made Artemis forget they were in the heart of a dangerous slum. A bonfire crackled and danced in the center of a small clearing, casting flickering shadows on the faces of the people gathered around it. Laughter and conversation filled the air, creating an atmosphere that was almost festive.

"Look over there," Forester whispered, nodding toward a group of men seated on makeshift stools, their attention focused on games of dice and backgammon. The clinking of tea glasses punctuated their animated conversations, and money exchanged hands with a fervor that spoke of the importance of every lira.

Artemis watched the scene with mixed emotions. On one hand, it was a welcome reprieve from the oppressive gloom of the slum, a reminder that even in the darkest places, people found ways to come together and enjoy life. But on the other hand, she couldn't help but feel like an intruder, a trespasser in a world she didn't belong in.

A few paces beyond these men, they discovered another cluster of people, faces illuminated by the flickering light from a small television set perched precariously atop a stack of wooden crates. The soccer match, or futbol as the locals called it, was playing on the screen had captured the attention of the residents gathered around it, their eyes riveted to the action, hands gesturing wildly as they shouted their opinions and encouragement at the players.

"Jim bum!" one kept yelling. "Jim bum!"

It took Artemis a second to realize what he was actually saying. Cimbom.

"Look at them," Forester said quietly, his voice tinged with a mix of amusement and fascination. "You'd think the fate of the world rested on this match."

"Maybe for them, it does," Artemis replied, her gaze drifting over the enraptured faces before refocusing on their surroundings. As skilled as she was at reading people, she knew better than to underestimate the importance of seemingly trivial things. To those living here, perhaps the game provided a much-needed escape from the harsh reality that surrounded t hem.

Her thoughts were interrupted when her keen eyes caught sight of something out of place—a man carrying a purse. He was tall and lean, with a gaunt face that looked like it had been chiseled from stone. His hair was a greasy mop of dirty blond strands that hung limply across his forehead, while his sunken eyes darted nervously back and forth as he moved through the crowd.

"Forester," she whispered, discreetly nodding in the man's direction. "Over there."

"Got him," Forester murmured, his eyes narrowing as he took in the suspicious figure. "He definitely doesn't fit in, does he?"

"No, he doesn't. Think that's Irem's purse?"

"Could be. GPS is directing us straight at the guy."

Artemis watched as the man slithered through the throng of people with an almost serpentine grace, his movements fluid and sinuous, contradicting his emaciated appearance. It was as if he were trying to blend in, but his very presence was a stark contrast to the warmth and camaraderie that permeated the atmosphere.

"Should we approach him?" Forester asked, his hand instinctively hovering near his weapon.

Artemis hesitated for a moment, her instincts warring with each other. "No," she decided finally, her gaze never leaving the man. "Not yet. Let's observe him for a bit longer."

"Alright." Forester leaned back against a nearby wall, doing his best to appear nonchalant as they continued to watch their potential lead.

As Artemis studied the man, she couldn't help but wonder what he was doing here—whether he was, in fact, connected to Irem Korkmaz's murder, or simply another lost soul seeking solace in the shadows of the slum.

The man with the purse glanced around furtively, his eyes darting from one person to another as if expecting trouble. His thin frame was draped in a tattered jacket that hung loose on his skeletal shoulders.

He looked like he was about ready to leave the place—he'd scanned the gathered folk once more but didn't seem to spot whoever he was looking for. Artemis followed him with her eyes as he began to ease away from the various fires coming from barrels or refuse piles. He snuck a coin off the table where some men were playing cards and then pocketed it before anyone else spotted it. Then he picked up his pace, moving even more quickly. The light from the fires began to fade, and the dark of the slum threatened to swallow him.

Artemis nudged Cameron, and the two of them moved hastily after the man with the purse.

"Excuse me," Artemis called out, trying to sound casual. "May I have a moment?"

The man's head whipped around, his eyes widening like a cornered animal.

He spotted her and looked puzzled briefly. Perhaps because she was speaking English, or perhaps because pretty strangers didn't often call out to him at night. At least not in this setting.

But then, his eyes roamed to Cameron, and he stiffened.

The man's dirty fingers tightened on the strap of his purse. He stared at them.

Forester commented, "The bag doesn't match your shoes."

"Ne diyorsun?" he snapped.

"Same to you," Forester replied.

In that instant, purse-man made a decision. He spun on his heel and bolted into the nearest alley, clutching the handbag tightly.

"Damn it!" Forester muttered under his breath, already lurching forward.

Artemis and Forester raced after the fleeing figure. The alleyways of the slum twisted and turned, forming a maze of narrow passages surrounded by makeshift dwellings. They dodged laundry lines sagging under the weight of damp clothes and sidestepped piles of discarded trash.

As they rounded a corner, a group of children playing with an old soccer ball blocked their path. Despite the late hour, the children seemed as energetic as they might be at noon. Artemis swerved to avoid them, skidding on the loose gravel beneath her feet. Her heart pounded in her chest, adrenaline surging through her veins.

"Forester, split up!" she called out, seeing that the alley forked ahead.

"Got it!" he replied, veering off down the left-hand passage.

Artemis took the right, hoping she had made the correct decision. The alley narrowed further, forcing her to sidle sideways between the corrugated metal walls. She prayed that Forester was closing in on the man from the other side.

"Where are you?" she muttered under her breath, scanning the dimly lit path for any sign of their quarry.

A shout came from her left, followed by the unmistakable sound of bodies colliding. Artemis' heart leaped into her throat as she pushed herself faster, desperate to reach Forester before it was too late.

"Forester!" she cried out, her voice strangled with fear and desperation. "Are you all right?"

"Artemis!" his voice echoed through the narrow passage. "I've got him cornered! Hurry!"

She sprinted around the final bend, her breath ragged and her muscles screaming in protest. There, at the end of the alley, she found Forester standing over the crumpled form of the man, his foot planted firmly on the purse.

The man muttered a few choice insults, shaking his head.

"I heard that," Cameron snapped.

"What did he say?" Artemis asked.

"No clue. But I heard it."

Artemis frowned at where the man groveled on the ground, still clutching the strap of the floral purse.

Forester bent double, plucked at the zipper, and pulled out a phone.

He held it up, then wriggled it.

"Irem's," he said, his voice cold. He hauled the man on the ground to his feet. "I don't care what damn language you wanna do it in, but you and I are gonna chat."

CHAPTER 6

THE GARDEN SHED NOW serving as their makeshift interrogation room was barely larger than a prison cell, its walls lined with rusty tools and half-empty bags of fertilizer. A single, weak bulb hung from the ceiling, casting long shadows across the cramped space. Artemis and Cameron sat at a makeshift table, their knees nearly touching beneath it, while the suspect slouched in a rickety chair on the other side. They had to be careful; they weren't working for the police, and this entire operation had to remain hush-hush.

The suspect's eyes darted between Artemis and Cameron, his sullen face betraying no emotion. He spoke in hushed, clipped phrases, the unfamiliar language rolling off his tongue like clattering marbles. Artemis furrowed her brow, trying to make sense of the words. She glanced at Cameron, who seemed equally lost.

"Can you understand him?" whispered Artemis, her coal-black hair framing her pretty features as she leaned closer to Cameron.

"Nothing," he admitted with a sigh. "You?"

He glanced back towards where Helen was leaning against the far wall.

Their father had been the one to procure this garden shed for their use—it was situated behind the pool, though, the pool was currently closed because of the late hour.

Their father had also been the one to rouse Helen from her sleep and draft her as temporary translator.

All of this felt so wrong, to Artemis. She'd worked on the same side as the FBI... but now, in a foreign country... She didn't even know the name of their intelligence service.

Helen watched it all with her usual, attentive gaze, her curly brown hair tied back in a loose ponytail. She offered the suspect a warm smile, her gentle disposition evident even in these circumstances. The man visibly relaxed under her grace, his shoulders dropping just slightly.

"Ask him about the purse," Forester instructed, his voice low and measured.

Helen translated the question, her voice soft yet firm, the foreign words flowing more easily from her lips. The suspect's eyes flicked between the three of them before he responded. His tone was cautious, almost fearful, but Artemis couldn't understand what he said.

"Did he admit to taking the purse?" Artemis asked, her impatience growing.

Helen hesitated, her eyes flickering with an uncertainty that worried Artemis. It was crucial that Helen remained focused and in control of her mental health.

"He says he just found the purse."

Artemis leaned forward, her coal-black hair falling over her shoulders as she scrutinized the suspect's face. She could see the perspiration on his forehead and hear the barely perceptible tremble in his voice. Cameron shifted his weight in the cramped space, his arms crossed in an attempt to appear unyielding.

"Found it, huh?" Artemis asked skeptically, her gaze unwavering. "Funny how you happened to find a purse that belonged to a dead woman."

Cameron nodded in agreement. "Seems like a pretty lucky find to me."

Helen translated their disbelief, and the suspect's sullen demeanor shifted into agitation. He stammered a response, his voice rising as he tried to defend himself. Helen listened carefully before translating his words back to them.

"He says he took the purse because he wanted to return it to the proper owner," she explained.

Artemis studied the man's face, her eyes searching for any hint of dishonesty. Of course, he was lying about his motives. But his fear seemed genuine.

"Ask him where he found the purse?" Artemis said.

The man balked at the question, hesitant, nervously nibbling at his lower lip.

This time, Artemis didn't need any translation, as the man simply shrugged one shoulder, and glanced off to the side, mumbling incoherently.

Helen repeated the question, and the man sighed, and responded, "Tamam... ama, bak sen bana..." He rattled something off so fast that Artemis glanced at her sister as if watching a tennis match.

Helen was frowning, and she said, "He admits that he found the purse near a body. But he says he didn't have anything to do with the death."

Artemis felt her excitement rising. Now they were getting somewhere.

The man looked nervous but defiant. She couldn't understand Turkish, but she knew human nature. She could read his body language, and he was glaring right at her now as if daring her to doubt him.

Either this was someone who truly believed what they were saying, or he was a masterful liar. It took a lot of training, like her father's, to know how to lie with both words and body.

"Ask him if he saw anyone else near the victim," she instructed Helen, her mind racing with possible scenarios while her exterior remained calm and collected.

As Helen conveyed the question, the suspect shook his head vehemently, his hands gripping the edge of the table. With each word he spoke, his desperation became more apparent, as if he was pleading with them to believe him.

"Please," he begged through Helen's translation, his eyes wide with fear. "I only took the purse because she didn't need it anymore. I wanted to feed my family."

The dim light cast eerie shadows across the cramped garden shed as Artemis leaned in closer to the suspect, her coal-black hair falling over her shoulders. She felt the weight of Helen's presence at her side, the essential link between them and the frightened man before them. Helen's curly brown hair framed her gentle face, a contrast to her sister's sharp features.

"Ask him if he searched the purse," Artemis said to Helen, her voice low and measured. Helen nodded and translated the question. The suspect hesitated, his fingers nervously tapping on the table. He glanced up at Artemis, then back down at his hands, before speaking. His words spilled out quickly, like water from a broken dam, and Artemis waited patiently for Helen to relay his response.

"He says he didn't search it thoroughly," Helen said softly. "He only checked for money and valuables."

Artemis studied the man a moment longer, then nodded; she reached for the purse, its fabric worn and stained, and slowly opened it. Perhaps there was something inside that the suspect had missed, something that could provide a clue to the identity of the killer—if this man was telling the truth, that was.

She hesitated, still half-peering into the purse, and realized she didn't think it was him.

Why would he have kept the purse on him? The phone in it?

The murder was gruesome, but meticulous.

The person had gone to great lengths to stage the body just-so. Would they have been foolish enough to keep something as damning as the victim's purse on their person?

She didn't think so.

Nodding, as if affirming her own silent counsel, she returned her attention to the handbag.

As she sifted through the contents, she found the items one might expect in a teenage girl's purse.

Lip gloss, a hairbrush, a wallet, and a cell phone. But something caught her eye, tucked away in the corner of the purse. It was a small, folded piece of paper. She carefully removed it from its hiding place and unfolded it.

Her fingers brushed against the crumpled piece of paper. Unfolding it, she discovered it was a paystub from a gambling hall. Curiosity piqued, Artemis examined it more closely, noting the date and amount.

"Ask him if he knows anything about this," she instructed Helen, holding up the paystub.

Helen conveyed the message, but the suspect shook his head, his confusion evident. While Helen translated his denial, Artemis's thoughts raced, considering the potential significance of the gambling hall connection.

"Could the victim have been involved in some sort of gambling debt?" she wondered aloud, voicing her thoughts for Cameron and Helen to hear.

Artemis held the paystub between her fingers, her eyes narrowing as she tried to make sense of the numbers printed on it. She could feel the weight of Cameron's gaze on her, and the uneasy silence that hung in the small space.

The small, dimly lit room seemed to shrink as the intensity of their interrogation grew. Artemis and Cameron sat across from the suspect, their focused gazes unwavering. A bead of sweat trickled down the man's forehead, his expression a mixture of fear and defiance.

"Ask him again about the paystub," Artemis said quietly, her piercing eyes scanning the table for any overlooked clue. "We need more information."

Helen relayed the question. The man hesitated, biting his lip nervously before responding in stilted words that Helen translated back to them.

"He says he doesn't know anything about it. He saw it in the purse but didn't think much of it."

"Really?" Artemis raised an eyebrow, her mind working quickly, like a Grandmaster analyzing a chessboard. "Helen, can you ask him if he has ever been to this gambling hall?"

As Helen translated, the suspect shook his head vehemently, insisting on his innocence. His sullen demeanor had given way to slight agitation, as if he knew how close they were to either accusing or exonerating him.

The suspect swallowed hard, and then slowly pulled out his phone. Helen translated his words in a hushed tone. "He says he has messages on his phone that he sent to a friend the night he found the purse. He's willing to show us if it helps."

"Let's see them," Artemis agreed, curiosity piqued.

As they scrolled through the messages, piecing together the story from the translated texts, Artemis could feel the puzzle pieces starting to fall into place.

In the texts, the man was frightened at first. He found a body, he'd texted. And then the purse.

It wasn't the texts of someone trying to create an alibi—nor were they the texts of someone who knew how to manage themselves in intense situations.

If anything, these texts put him directly at the scene of the crime.

The purse tied him to the victim.

But as Artemis studied the man, she realized—with a sinking sensation—she believed his innocence.

At least of the murder.

No... something else was going on here.

Something far more than just a mugging gone wrong.

If the man was after the purse, why go to the trouble of drowning the victim the way it had happened.

Artemis shivered, shaking her head and biting her lip.

It felt as if a chill breeze crept through the room as she rocked back on her heels.

She paced around the table, staring at the paystub centering the metal.

"Thoughts?" Forester directed his gaze towards her.

"Let him go," she whispered.

"Really?"

"Yes."

Forester shrugged, and pulled the man to his feet, pushing him towards the door.

The purse thief hesitated, staring, slack-jawed. His features had been pale up to now, as if the blood had drained from them, but as he realized he was being pushed towards the door, his eyes widened in relief.

He stammered a few quick words as he was pushed out into the night by Cameron.

Forester paused in the doorway, glancing back. "I'll make sure he leaves."

Artemis nodded, staring at where the tall man was framed by the moon.

"We need to visit that gambling hall," she said.

Forester nodded. "Are you thinking what I'm thinking?"

Sighing, Artemis's lips drew into a worried frown. "People kill over money all the time. Debts. Simple greed. Revenge if they feel cheated. It's a statement."

"The murder looked like a message," Forester agreed. "The sort a bookie might send."

"Exactly," Artemis replied.

She frowned, plucking the piece of paper off the table, and staring at it. A gambling hall—especially the sort that allowed seventeen-year-olds—wasn't exactly a safe location to visit.

But she'd already resigned herself to the likelihood of danger.

She could only hope this 'fresh start' in Istanbul didn't result in the death of anyone she loved.

CHAPTER 7

THERE WAS NO REST for the wicked, and the dead of night was no reprieve for Artemis Blythe. She stared at the aforementioned wicked, where they'd gathered in the small confines of a bar under a neon sign.

Late-night Istanbul was a world of its own, teeming with activity and the promise of danger. The dim streetlights cast an eerie glow over the narrow cobblestone streets, their shadows mingling with those of the figures that moved stealthily in the darkness. As the faint sound of music and laughter filled the air, Artemis stood at a safe distance, taking in the scene before her.

"Forester," she whispered, "there must be at least half a dozen guards around the entrance."

"Seems they're not taking any chances tonight," Forester replied gruffly, his eyes scanning the area as he flexed his scarred palm. His disheveled hair and clothing made him blend seamlessly into the dark alleyway.

Artemis' plain and simple attire allowed her to blend into the shadows as well.

"Let's try the back," Artemis suggested, her voice barely audible above the bustling atmosphere of the Turkish gambling ring. The two began to move cautiously through the alley, keeping close to the walls and avoiding the pools of light from the windows above them.

As they got closer to the main building, the din of the gambling floor grew louder, the energy almost palpable even outside the thick, stone walls.

"Look out!" Forester suddenly hissed, pushing Artemis against the wall to avoid being seen by a pair of wandering guards. They held their breaths, watching as the guards moved past them, chatting animatedly to each other.

Once they were gone, Artemis and Forester continued their way through the alley.

As they approached the back of the building, it became clear that gaining entry without being seen would be difficult. The windows were situated high up on the walls, and the doors were heavily guarded.

Artemis eyed the window above her, calculating the distance and the leverage she would need.

"Keep watch," she whispered to Forester, who nodded silently, his eyes scanning the alley for any potential threats.

After a quick survey of the alley, she snatched up a small, rusted butter knife next to a trashcan and pushed off the small, brick fence to reach the window.

Perched precariously on a narrow ledge, Artemis slipped the blade of the knife between the window frame and the pane, hoping to pry it open without drawing attention to herself. The metal groaned softly under the pressure, but she gritted her teeth, sweat beading on her forehead as she focused on the task at hand.

"Come on..." she muttered, frustration mounting with each passing second.

Just as the window began to give way, a sudden movement caught Artemis's eye.

She nearly fell and yelped, catching herself by bracing against the window, and leaving streaks of fingerprints on the glass.

Four men emerged from the shadows, each armed with a crowbar, their faces hidden beneath low-slung hats. Artemis froze, her heart hammering in her chest as she tried to calculate their intentions.

"Forester," she murmured, her voice barely audible as she maintained her grip on the knife, ready to defend herself if necessary. "We've got company."

"Stay calm," he replied through clenched teeth, keeping his eyes fixed on the approaching figures. "I'll handle this."

Artemis hesitated, torn between trusting Forester's expertise and her own instincts.

"Alright," she agreed reluctantly, focusing her attention back on the window. "Just be careful."

"Always am," he replied, taking a step forward to meet the men head-on.

As Artemis continued her struggle with the stubborn window frame, she couldn't help but worry for Forester's safety. He was skilled, yes, but four against one were odds that even the most talented fighter would find challenging.

She continued to pry at the window, though.

Artemis glanced at the alley mouth, her loose hair falling into her eyes as she worked the knife into the window frame. She hesitated, considering the four burly men armed with crowbars who now blocked their path.

It was an odd choice, she realized, to continue work on the window as if the scene below were of no concern.

She was concerned. Very.

But she also knew Cameron Forester.

He'd once been a cage-fighter, and he was currently armed.

But the gun remained holstered as he faced the four men.

She felt her stomach twist.

Forester stepped forward, closing the distance between himself and the men. He cracked his knuckles, a small smile playing on his lips as he regarded his opponents. "You boys really shouldn't be here," he said conversationally, as though discussing the weather rather than preparing for a fight.

One of the men growled, brandishing his crowbar menacingly.

"Ah, well," Forester shrugged, "I suppose we all make mistakes, don't we?"

With that, he launched himself at the first man, ducking under a wild swing and delivering a powerful blow to the man's mid-section. The attacker doubled over, gasping for air, and Forester pivoted gracefully to face the next.

"Come on" Artemis whispered again, her fingers slipping on the handle of the knife. The window finally gave way with a soft groan, and she quickly pushed it open, her pulse racing as she considered their next move.

"Forester!" she called urgently, "It's open! Let's go!"

"Right behind you" he grunted, delivering a swift punch to another man.

A crowbar swung at his head, but he danced out of the way.

Now that she was paying closer attention, she realized the four men were all wearing the same black suits.

Forester continued to fight, his movements fluid and precise as he wove through the four attackers. He blocked and parried, each punch and kick delivered with calculated precision.

One man with a crowbar swung again, but this time Forester was ready. He grabbed the weapon mid-swing, jerking it out of the man's grip before delivering a sharp jab to his chin. The man stumbled back, joining his three companions on the ground in a crumpled heap.

Artemis stared at them, then feeling vindicated about her choice to work on the window, she called out, "Come on!"

"Sorry, am I too slow for you?" he called back.

She frowned, still perched on the ledge, one hand still bracing the window open.

Forester pointed at the pile of men. One of the thugs, groaning, was starting to rise, and Cameron gave him a light love tap, sending him back to sleep.

"See?" he called out, pointing. "I did this. Takes time."

It was as if he were displaying a work of art or a construction paper painting to be hung on the fridge.

"Well, come on! More will come!"

The sounds from the gambling hall hadn't changed. The laughter, the clinking of drinks, and the faint music of stringed instruments thrumming inside still blocked out most of the noise from the alley.

She clicked her fingers, gesturing at him again.

With the last of the men now lying unconscious on the ground, Forester wiped the sweat from his brow and nodded in approval as Artemis slipped through the open window. The moon cast an eerie glow upon her face as she carefully reached out and pulled him into the dimly lit room.

"Nice work," Forester whispered, his eyes scanning their surroundings, ever vigilant.

They were in a foul-smelling, Turkish bathroom.

Artemis wrinkled her nose in disgust at the pungent odor. "I think we're in the wrong place," she muttered, her eyes scanning the cramped space for any clues as to where they were supposed to go.

Forester nodded, his hand hovering over the handle of his gun as he listened for any signs of danger. "The bookies should be here somewhere."

Artemis nodded as they crept through the narrow, dimly lit room, and immediately out into a corridor, equally poorly lit. They moved silently, their footsteps muffled by the old, worn carpet beneath their feet.

As they turned a corner, they heard the sound of voices echoing from a nearby room.

The corridor opened up into a larger room, the door propped open. Within, they spotted where a man sat at a computer with his back to them, completely unaware of their presence. A one-way window beside him revealed the bustling gambling hall just beyond him: men and women huddled around roulette wheels and card tables, their faces etched with determination and desperation.

"Excuse me," Forester announced, his voice booming across the small room as he tapped the man on the shoulder. The fellow behind the glass turned around in surprise, his face a mixture of shock and fear.

"Who the hell are you?" he demanded, attempting to muster some semblance of authority.

It took a second for Artemis to realize he was speaking nearly flawless English.

She also decided this was mostly definitely the bookie. Everything on his desk from the stacks of cash to the betting slips strewn about confirmed it.

The bookie's fingers twitched towards the cellphone on his desk, sweat beading on his forehead. Forester's eyes narrowed, and in a swift motion, he knocked the phone away with a cracking noise, sending it skittering across the floor.

"Ah, I wouldn't do that if I were you," Forester warned, his voice low and menacing, like the growl of a wolf. The bookie swallowed hard, his Adam's apple bobbing nervously, as he raised his hands in an attempt to placate the intruders.

"Alright, alright," he stammered. "But just so you know, hurting me won't clear your debt. I'm just the messenger."

She wondered at his English for a second but then realized as someone who worked in one of the most tourist-visited cities in the world, not knowing the language in this establishment would've been a missed business opportunity.

Artemis stood by, her heart thudding loudly in her ears as she watched Forester loom over the bookie.

"Tell us about Irem Korkmaz," Forester demanded, his voice unwavering.

"Do you have any idea whose place this is? Mehmet is gonna eat you alive when he—"

Forester shoved a finger to the man's lips, smooshing his face a little as he interrupted him. "Don't care. Don't care about any of that. Irem Korkmaz. Tell me what you know before I crack your head open on that desk and start rooting around in there for the answer myself."

"Korkmaz?" the bookie repeated hesitantly, beads of sweat forming on his brow. "I... don't recognize the name."

"Don't lie."

"I don't!" he squeaked.

Artemis stepped forward. "So you didn't hear what happened to her this morning?"

"Happened?"

"Irem is dead."

He just shook his head. "I... I'm sorry, but what does this have to do with me?"

"Irem Korkmaz was a seventeen-year-old girl," Forester snapped. He often got angry where young women were involved. He had a soft spot for them, and a protective streak Artemis believed went back to his late wife.

"I... Oh, the Bosphorus murder?" the bookie said suddenly, his voice quiet.

"Speak up!" Forester snapped, his impatience palpable.

"I... I may actually remember. Yes! Y-yes, she was trying to pay off her father's gambling debt," the bookie admitted, his voice trembling with anxiety. "She seemed desperate—said she would do anything to clear his name. I-I don't know much more than that."

As Artemis listened to the bookie's words, a mixture of pity and anger settled in her chest. She imagined the fear and helplessness Irem must have felt.

"Her father's debt?" Artemis said.

"Yes. She had a pay stub from him. She said they couldn't afford it." He nodded quickly.

"Let me guess," Forester said. "You were a nice guy and waived any debt, right?"

"I... I didn't have that sort of authority," the small man protested, nervously blinking behind his wire-frame glasses. He shrugged. "Besides, her father... He isn't the sort that will stop coming just because his daughter trades something for his debt."

"Trades?" Forester. "I don't like the sound of that."

The bookie squeaked. "Nothing illicit! This is a business. I help with a business. That's all. Mr. Mehmet is very particular about keeping things... professional."

He glanced towards the door, likely searching for the guards Forester had put to sleep.

"Alright," Cameron said. "So she was here?"

"Very briefly. Yes. Who... who are you?"

"CIA," Cameron lied. "When she was here, what then?"

"I told you. She begged for the debt to be waved. I said no. She promised to find a way to pay it. Simple as that."

"So she paid it?" Artemis interjected.

"No. But she said she knew how. She just had to speak to her father. A very foolish move, if you ask me." He snorted, tugging at the sleeves of his jacket.

"Why foolish?" Cameron asked.

The bookie's eyes darted nervously between them, and then he swallowed hard.

"Her father, Osman Korkmaz... He's not someone you want to mess with. The man's dangerous. Very dangerous," he warned, beads of perspiration forming on his forehead.

"Elaborate," Forester urged, his scarred palm flexing around the grip of his gun.

"Osman has a temper—a violent one," the bookie continued, visibly frightened. "When people cross him, they have a habit of disappearing."

Artemis felt a chill run down her spine at the mention of Irem's father, but she quickly masked her emotions as she processed the information.

"In fact," the bookie said, realizing he'd said something that had them interested. "From what I've heard, Osman once beat a man to death with his bare hands... No... no, wait. Ah, that's right. He beat him then drowned him."

Artemis and Forester shared a look.

Suddenly, they heard the sound of shouting. Of heavy foot-steps.

"Shit," Cameron said. "Let's go, Art."

She was already moving. The two of them hastening away from the bespectacled bookie.

If he was telling the truth, then he had no reason to hurt Irem.

She was supposed to pay a debt.

But if Irem's father had a history of violence?

Of drowning...

Artemis felt a cold shiver down her spine as she hurried away with Forester, moving through the desolate hall and away from the sound of angry voices and rushing footsteps.

CHAPTER 8

ARTEMIS FLOPPED ONTO THE bed, staring at the ceiling and feeling the weight of exhaustion heavy on her shoulders. She let out a leaking sigh and tried to close her eyes, but it was almost as if her eyelids were too heavy to even close.

They'd decided to wait before confronting Osman Kormaz.

She let out a faint breath, inhaling through her nose and out through her mouth.

She tried to refocus on her thoughts—to process the night's events.

"Another case," she whispered under her breath.

She wasn't sure if she was upset.

Perhaps, it was more that she was upset by how she wasn't upset.

She wrinkled her nose as these thoughts whisked through her mind as fast as her synapses could fire.

They'd come to Turkey for a fresh start.

The city had promised lax extradition laws and the ability to avoid the ghosts that haunted Seattle.

But there were murders here too...

She stared at the door which led out into the small apartment unit.

The money they'd received from rescuing a billionaire's daughter was more than enough to cover the place, but she hadn't wanted to show up in a foreign country just tossing cash around.

Still... Eventually, a bigger place was in order.

She managed to close her eyes, picturing Izel in her mind. The girl had been so sad at the death of her friend.

But Irem...

Irem had been drowned. A rope around her ankle... and then dragged back on deck and left to be discovered like day-old refuse.

Artemis frowned now. She thought of how Forester often reacted to these situations, and her hand bunched up on the bed, gripping a handful of sheets.

Cameron often got protective where young women were concerned.

He'd certainly been that way with her, and her mind moved to Forester's wife...

She frowned and sat up.

How come she couldn't remember the woman's name?

Had Cameron once told her?

K... something?

Artemis shook her head. Had she never asked? Or had she blocked out the name?

She frowned, feeling strangely uncomfortable now, sitting cross-legged on the bed, her mind moving rapidly.

She stared at the door.

For a brief moment, she considered letting the matter go.

She needed her sleep.

But then she pushed to her feet, hastened to her door, and stepped out into the dark hall of their new apartment in the gated community.

The walls were bare. The floors were clean but padded with linoleum.

The scent of air freshener—lilac—lingered in the room.

Artemis hastened down the hall, past two doors—bathroom and Helen's—then reached the door at the far end.

She pressed her ear against the door, listening.

No sound.

Was Cameron asleep?

She raised her hand to knock, when a voice said, "He's not in there."

She turned sharply.

Her father was sitting up on the couch, where he'd chosen to sleep. His covers were bunched at his legs, and his back was straight. He stared at her like some riddling Sphinx, his eyes bright and pale like moonlight.

"He's not there," her father repeated.

She frowned and pushed open the door to Cameron's room.

Empty.

"He went for a walk; said he couldn't sleep," Otto supplied, still watching his daughter.

Somehow, the middle-aged man's golden, curled hair still looked immaculate despite the fact that he'd been apparently sleeping only seconds before.

"You keeping tabs on everyone?" she asked.

She hadn't meant it to sound so hostile.

"No. Light sleeper. Effect of prison," he said simply.

She winced. "I see..."

She wasn't sure if it was intentional, but both of their gazes darted to the door to Helen's room. Both of them likely thinking similar thoughts.

Helen was the cause of her father's prison time.

"I don't know if I ever thanked you properly," Artemis said quietly. She glanced back at Otto.

Her father had always been a hard man to read. Where he sat on the couch, he almost seemed like a stone gargoyle, his countenance like granite.

"For what?" he said.

"For what you did for Helen."

"She's my daughter, Artemis. I would've done the same for you."

"Really?"

"I moved here, didn't I?"

She wanted to point out that he'd had nowhere left to go but decided this would have sounded churlish.

So instead, she said, "I'm not sure I could've done it. Spent all that time in prison for a crime I didn't commit."

Her father just watched her, but then gave a brief shake of his head. "I believe you would've done the same," he said simply.

Artemis nodded slowly, not entirely sure if she agreed, but not wanting to argue either. She turned to leave but then paused, looking back at Otto. "What do you think about the case?" she asked, her voice low.

Otto's eyes narrowed slightly. "Which case?"

"The murder. Wait, what other case is there?"

"Depends who you ask. But I think we need to be careful," Otto said after a moment. "This is not our country. We do not know who we can trust."

Artemis nodded, knowing he was right. "What about Cameron?" she asked, her tone softer now.

"I trust him," Otto said simply.

Artemis nodded again, feeling a weight lift off her shoulders. It was good to hear that Otto felt the same way. She turned to leave but then paused again. "You're not going to tell him I came looking for him, are you?" she asked with a half-smile. "He would never let me hear the end of it."

Otto's lips twitched in response. "No, I think I can keep that a secret," he said, his voice dry.

Artemis grinned, feeling a sense of camaraderie with her father that she hadn't felt in a long time. She left the living room and made her way back to her own bedroom. She crawled back onto the bed, feeling more exhausted than ever but also more at ease.

Somewhere, deep in her subconscious, she pictured the car that had been following her and Helen only the previous week.

It had been Helen's idea to buy the fake ticket...

But why?

No one had been tracking them...

No one was after them...

At least not yet.

The FBI didn't know Helen's actions. They didn't know Otto was with his daughters.

Artemis shook her head, pushing aside any further troubling thoughts.

Tomorrow morning, they'd have enough trouble. Osman Korkmaz was apparently a violent man. A dangerous one.

She wasn't sure how confronting a man like this about his own daughter's murder would go.

She closed her eyes, letting her thoughts drift, and finally, she fell into a deep sleep.

CHAPTER 9

"So I HEAR YOU came looking for me," Cameron said conversationally, sitting in the front of their rental car.

She looked sharply at him. "What?"

"Last night," he said, smirking.

She glared through the windshield at the small house ahead of them. "My dad can't keep his mouth shut."

"He didn't tell me."

"Helen?"

"Nah," he smirked. "I was on the roof, but my window was open. Could hear it."

She glared at him. "Well... good thing I didn't find you. I might've had to slap that stupid smirk off your stupid face."

"Doubly stupid? Damn. You know what they say, though. Ignorance is bliss."

"I think the real saying is—"

But before she could finish, Cameron leaned in, stole a kiss, and then pushed out of the car, leaving her gaping after him like a landed fish.

She closed her mouth, opened it again, and then frowned.

Then, muttering to herself about impertinence, Artemis also pushed out of the vehicle to face Osman Korkmaz's small, dilapidated house on the outskirts of Istanbul's Pendik bazaar district.

As they approached the house, Artemis could feel her heart pounding in her chest. She had a feeling that this was not going to be an easy conversation. She had dealt with criminals before, but Osman Korkmaz was different. He was a murderer according to the bookie, and they were about to ask him about potentially being involved in his own daughter's death whether implicitly or complicitly.

Cameron walked beside her, his hand brushing against hers. She took a deep breath. They reached the front door and Cameron knocked.

After a few moments, the door creaked open to reveal an older man with a thick mustache and deep-set wrinkles. He looked them up and down, his eyes narrowing.

"Ne istiyorsun?" he snapped.

Artemis stepped forward, her voice steady. "Mr. Korkmaz, we need to talk to you about your daughter's death." She winced. Realizing she'd spoken too fast. She said, slowly, "Irem. Irem Korkmaz."

At his daughter's name, the man's face turned red, his eyes flashing with anger. "You know Irem?"

He spoke in broken English, the words grasped for hesitantly.

Artemis blinked in surprise. She'd found out that Osman had attended Uskudar Academy in his youth, across the Bosphorus—an elite school that taught in English. But he'd been kicked out, and it had been two decades ago.

She had only *hoped* the man had maintained his English—and to call what he spoke English, was somewhat generous—but he seemed to understand what they wanted well enough.

"We didn't know her personally," Artemis said slowly. "But we're looking into her murder."

"Murder?" he said, wrinkling his nose as if unfamiliar with the word.

"Death," Artemis said.

He frowned again. "Yes. Dead. Today."

"Yesterday," Forester provided.

"Yes. Yesterday."

Artemis glanced at her partner, then back at the man in the door. He didn't look nearly as intimidating as she'd been told to believe.

She could see the anger simmering in his gaze, though. He had a bit of a belly, suggesting an affinity for beverage consumption of the alcoholic variety.

His face was red, and behind him, in the house, she spotted more than one bottle scattered across the ground.

But as she spoke, slowly, she found herself less timid, and a bit more gentle.

"I'm very sorry for your loss, sir."

"Mhmm." He just nodded.

Now, he looked bored. He had hooked the door with one heel and was beginning to close it.

"We'd like to help!" Artemis said quickly.

The door was still closing. She felt desperate and called out, "Please! Sir—we need to know if you know anything."

The door was almost shut, but Cameron jammed his foot to stop it. "Hey, pal, we're trying to help."

The man glared at the foot then up at Cameron. He began to speak, but then he spotted Cameron's lumpy, fighter's ear. He stopped, holding his tongue as if thinking better of it.

The two men now glared at each other, and Artemis feared they were on the verge of exchanging blows. She quickly said, "Please! Izel sent us!"

At the name of his daughter's dear friend, Osman hesitated. "Izel?" he asked.

"Yes! Yes, Izel asked us to help."

"How know Izel?"

"Chess," Artemis said quickly. "She saw me play chess once."

"Satranc?"

"What?"

"Chess."

"Yes!" Artemis said, wincing hopefully.

Osman was still glaring at the foot blocking his door, but then he sighed, shrugged, and stepped back, gesturing for them to enter his house. As Forester stepped in first, Osman burped and seemed to intentionally direct the fragrant breeze in Cameron's direction.

Artemis followed Forester inside, trying to ignore the smell of alcohol and the mess everywhere. The walls were bare, devoid of any decorations, and the furniture looked like it had seen better days. The only source of light came from a small table lamp in the corner.

Once inside, Osman motioned for them to sit at a small table, and he took a seat opposite them.

"Irem," he said, his voice thick with emotion. "She was good girl. Smart. Work hard. Want be doctor."

Artemis felt a pang of sympathy for the man. Losing a child was never easy. "We're sorry for your loss," she said softly.

Osman nodded, his eyes misty. "You find who do this?"

"We're trying to," Artemis said. "Do you have any ideas? Anything that might help us?"

She felt her gaze fixating on the side of his face. His betting slip had been found in his daughter's purse. His gambling had led to said daughter visiting a dangerous gambling hall. Was that what had eventually cost Irem her life? Artemis didn't think it wise to lead by strong-arming the man. So she spoke quietly, keeping her tone in check and devoid of any accusation.

He shook his head. "No. Irem work hard, study. Keep to self."

"Did she have any enemies?" Cameron asked, leaning forward.

Osman frowned, rubbing his chin. "No. No enemies. Irem good girl."

Artemis exchanged a look with Forester. This wasn't getting them anywhere.

"Did she have a boyfriend?" Forester asked, trying a different angle.

Osman shook his head. "No. Irem no boyfriend. Too busy."

Artemis sighed. "And what can you tell us about the Ahududu Gambling Hall?"

He looked up sharply, recognition in his gaze.

He looked like a sad, tired, defeated old man. The warnings they'd heard of his temper, his violent nature, were either unfounded or exaggerated.

Or perhaps just lurking beneath the surface. People were not always what they initially seemed.

He had gone still at the mention of the gambling hall, and then glanced at Forester, then back at Artemis.

For a moment, his eyes seemed to clear, and a shrewd look—which seemed as if it belonged there—crossed his gaze.

"Who are you?" he said slowly, a sly note creeping into his tone.

"We told you, we're here as a favor to Izel."

He licked his lips carefully, then reached slowly—as if stretching—under the table.

She spotted the way he was moving and shot a quick glance at Forester in warning.

Cameron stepped forward, frowning and holding out a hand towards Mr. Korkmaz.

"They sent you, didn't they?" Osman said slowly.

"Who's they?" Cameron said.

But Osman's hand was still under the table, hidden from sight. His eyes darted back and forth between the two of them once more, and he looked as if he were inching back.

Artemis could feel the tension in the room mounting with every second Osman's hand remained hidden under the table. She exchanged a worried glance with Forester, silently communicating her concern. Cameron, on the other hand, seemed unfazed. He stood in front of the table, his arms crossed, and his expression unreadable.

"Who sent you?" Osman repeated, his eyes darting back and forth between Artemis and Cameron. "I know they watch me. They always are."

Artemis was starting to feel uneasy. The man's behavior was erratic, and she wasn't sure how much longer they could keep him talking before he did something unpredictable. She took a deep breath and tried to remain calm.

"Izel sent us," she said slowly, keeping her tone gentle. "She's worried about your daughter. I'm sure she's worried about you too."

Osman snorted. "I don't need help," he muttered. "I take care of self."

Artemis knew this was a lie. The man was clearly in distress, and his daughter's murder had left him vulnerable. She glanced at Forester, silently urging him to intervene.

"Mr. Korkmaz," Forester said, his voice firm. "We're here to help. We want to find out who killed your daughter. But we can't do that if you don't cooperate with us."

Osman's hand remained under the table, but Artemis could see the tension in his shoulders easing slightly. He seemed to be considering their words.

But then he looked at Cameron Forester as if taking in the man's large frame for the first time. Cameron was an acquired taste—and at first glance, he was a frightening specimen. he towered over most, and his muscles seemed to have muscles of their own.

The array of scars and tattoos didn't help anything either.

He swallowed and frowned again. "You were sent to collect my debt?"

"No," Artemis said firmly. She could tell he was trying to excite himself into some form of action. "We're not with the gambling hall. We're not—"

But the mention of the word 'gambling' seemed to do it again. His eyes widened, and he released a sudden screech.

He whipped his hand out from under the table, holding a knife.

He slashed it towards Cameron, but Forester moved quickly, his eyes never leaving Osman's. In a swift motion, he placed a hand on the man's wrist and with his free hand twisted, prying the knife from his grasp. Then he stepped back and set it down on the table, out of reach.

It was all over in a second.

Osman blinked, stared at the knife, and then he seemed to deflate in front of them, all of his energy suddenly gone. He looked up at Forester with a mixture of fear and resignation in his eyes.

"Sit down," Forester said quietly, guiding him back into his seat.

Once Osman was safely seated again, Forester took a step back and crossed his arms over his chest. His expression had grown darker now, more accusatory than before.

"Now," he said gruffly. "Did your gambling debt get your daughter killed?"

"Wh-what?"

"She went to the hall. She spoke to your bookie."

Osman looked like he'd been slapped. "What?" he whispered.

"It's true," Artemis said. "We spoke to the bookie last night. He remembered your daughter."

Osman was now rocking back and forth in his wooden chair, the legs of the furniture piece scraping against the ground. He spoke again in his worn and broken English, his heavy accent only getting worse as grief filled his voice.

"I didn't know," he said hoarsely. "She never told me she went there. I wish—stopped her if I knew."

Artemis and Forester exchanged a look, both of them wondering if they could believe Osman's words.

"I didn't know," he said, his eyes filling with tears. "I didn't know she went there. I thought she was studying, working hard. I didn't know she had gamble."

Artemis felt a pang of sympathy for the man. "Sir... she wasn't there to gamble. She was there to clear your debt."

She said it as calmly, as carefully as she could, but the moment she'd spoken, she could tell her words had floored the man.

He gaped at her and then hung his head in his hands.

His shoulders began shaking and sitting there in that worn kitchen with the old furniture, he had the look of a candle that had just been pinched out, the last thin traces of fire disappearing from him like a thin curl of translucent smoke.

"How much did you owe them?" Artemis said. "That section of the bet slip was cut off."

"What? Bet what?"

"Slip. Just how much did you owe?" she pressed a bit more firmly.

"I don't know in dollar."

"In lira is fine," she replied.

He looked like he was struggling to remember. "Five thousand," he finally said, his voice barely above a whisper.

Forester let out a low whistle. "That's a lot of money."

"It was, how you say... loan," Osman said, his voice breaking. "I thought I win it back."

"How'd that work out for ya?" Forester said.

Artemis shot him a look, frowning. But Cameron didn't seem at all taken with the man's demeanor. If anything, Cameron looked accusatory.

Artemis just sighed, massaging the bridge of her nose. "So you didn't know about your daughter trying to clear your debt?"

He gave an adamant shake of his head.

"And if you had known, what would you have done?" Forester said firmly.

"Done?"

"Yes. Done."

"Nothing."

"Sure... Keep telling yourself that, bud."

Osman tried to stand up, but Forester pushed him hard.

"Cut the act."

"Cameron!" Artemis said, warning him. But Forester ignored her.

He was pointing a finger at the man by the kitchen table.

"You're not the victim here, asshole. Your daughter is. And I have half a mind to toss your place and see if you had anything to do with this shit. You're the one who was gambling, and now you're drunk as hell."

"Cameron," Artemis said urgently, trying to tug him back, but Forester was no longer listening.

His anger was palpable, and it almost felt personal to him. "So tell us something useful, or I'm going to start breaking things. Not that you've got shit in this place that's worth much."

Osman just gaped at the large, ex-fighter.

In response, Cameron picked up one of the chairs and smashed it.

"Cameron! Stop!" Artemis tried to interject, but he was moving over a bottle by the counter.

"Wait!" protested Osman.

"Oh, I see," Cameron snapped. "Finally found something you care about, huh?"

Cameron smashed the half-empty bottle against the sink. the glass shattered, and small pieces scattered across the ground.

Cameron's hand was bleeding, but he didn't even seem to notice. He raised the bloody hand, pointing a finger at Osman. "Well? Do I have to keep searching? What about that television over there? Looks like it gets good use, huh?"

Osman was on his feet but looked downright terrified.

Artemis wasn't sure what had gotten into Cameron, but she stepped forward, trying to intervene, standing in front of him before he could move toward the TV.

He was breathing heavily, his muscled chest rising and falling rapidly. "Wait!" Osman protested. "Wait... Okay. Listen."

Cameron let go of the glass bottle he'd been aiming towards the television. "I'm listening!"

"I... maybe. Irem good girl. But she might..." he trailed off, wincing.

"Might what?" Artemis said, frowning.

Osman had a look in his eyes. And he shifted uncomfortably from one foot to the other. "She... does boyfriend."

"What?" Cameron said.

"You said she doesn't have one," Artemis pointed out.

"Does. Did. Yes. She did have boyfriend."

"So?" Artemis said.

"His family. Honor."

"Honor?" Artemis said. And she remembered the mention of the police lead on honor killings.

She felt her stomach sink. Were they following leads a thousand steps behind the regular authorities? What if the police had it right, and all of this had been for nothing?

"You think her ex-boyfriend might have killed her?" she asked hesitantly.

He shrugged and hung his head, still looking weary.

Artemis and Forester exchanged a look. This was a new lead, and it was something they could work with.

"Tell us more about the boyfriend," Forester said, his voice firm.

Osman looked up at them, his eyes filled with sorrow. "His family... they no like of Irem. They thought she too West."

"Westernized?"

"Mhmm. They want her marry someone from village, someone they trust."

Artemis frowned. "Did they threaten her?"

Osman nodded. "Yes. They threat to harm."

"So where is this ex-boyfriend now?" Forester asked.

"He moved back to his village," Osman replied.

Artemis frowned. "Does he have a name?"

"Barish Esmer."

"And are there others in Barish's family who were threatening Irem?"

"Yes."

"Who?"

He shrugged. "All."

"All? What do you mean?" Cameron said.

But Artemis put a hand out, touching his arm, still trying to calm him and figure out what had caused his sudden outburst. She said, softly, "I think he means that all of the family were threatening her."

Osman nodded. He held up ten fingers. Then did it again. Then nodded before dipping his head and holding it.

Artemis tugged at Cameron's arm again.

He seemed loath to leave, but after a look of contempt directed towards their unwitting witness, he harumphed then turned, marching for the door.

He had only taken a few steps, though, before there were sudden shouts.

"Ellerinizi Yukselin!"

The door splintered, kicked in by a jack boot.

Five large men, wearing police uniforms, flashing badges and waving guns, burst through the door. Shouting a series of commands Artemis couldn't translate, but she completely understood.

Her hands found the air, but her stomach found her feet.

She dropped to her knees, and Forester went down next to her.

It was all a blur of color and motion as the cops circled them, and cuffs *clicked* into place, the metal cold against Artemis' skin.

It all happened so fast, it took a couple seconds for Artemis to realize just how much trouble they were in.

CHAPTER 10

SEATED IN THE DIMLY lit interrogation room, Artemis studied the rivets on the cold metal table, her hands cuffed to its sides. The air was thick with tension as she tried to calculate her next move.

The door creaked open and two Turkish interrogators entered the room. The male interrogator was a stern, middle-aged man with a neatly trimmed mustache wearing a crisp suit that screamed authority. He exuded an air of confidence, his steps precise and measured as he approached Artemis. Meanwhile, the female interrogator was younger, her piercing eyes promising a no-nonsense demeanor. She crossed her arms and sized up Artemis as if trying to read her thoughts.

"Miss Artemis," the male interrogator began in accented English, "We have some questions for you regarding the recent incident."

Artemis stared back at him, her gaze unwavering. She knew she had to tread carefully, her family's safety hinged on every word she uttered in this room.

"Ask away," she replied coolly.

The female interrogator leaned forward, her icy blue eyes narrowing. "You were seen in the vicinity of the Ahududu, a gambling hall. What were you doing there?"

"I was just passing by," Artemis said smoothly, her mind working overtime to craft a believable alibi.

The male interrogator raised an eyebrow, skeptical of her response. "Just passing by? That area is known for its criminal activity. It seems rather unlikely that an innocent bystander would simply be 'passing by.'"

"Maybe I took a wrong turn," Artemis countered, feigning nonchalance. But inside, her heart raced as she gauged their reactions, searching for any signs of disbelief.

"Or maybe you're involved in this mess," the female interrogator suggested, her tone sharp and accusatory.

"What mess is that?" Artemis asked.

She wasn't stalling—she really needed to know. Did this have to do with the murder? The gambling hall? Something else.

After she and Forester had been jammed into a police car, driven down a dusty road, and split into two separate interrogation rooms, she'd been left in silence until this very moment.

She didn't know why they'd been arrested or if the cops had been after them or after Osman.

"Fine," the female interrogator said, her voice dripping with disdain. "Tell us about your relationship with the victim."

The victim.

Shit.

This was about the murder.

Artemis glanced at the two interrogators, their faces a mix of frustration and suspicion. She knew she was playing a dangerous game, but she couldn't afford to lose.

Artemis's pulse quickened as the female interrogator leaned in, her cold gaze demanding answers. She felt a bead of sweat forming on her temple, betraying the unnerving effect of the woman's scrutiny.

"If you won't answer that, then tell us more about your relationship with Cameron Forester," the interrogator insisted, her voice as sharp as a knife.

"He's a friend."

"Is that so?" The female interrogator's eyebrows arched skeptically. "You expect us to believe that a man you call a friend went to great lengths to defend you outside a gambling hall, and yet you know nothing about his criminal activities?"

"What about the gambling hall?"

"He hospitalized two men. Another won't walk for a week."

Artemis nodded hesitantly, trying to keep her thoughts in check. "I'm sorry to hear it."

"Did Cameron put you up to it? Is that why Irem is dead?'

"Excuse me?"

"You know why you're here, Ms. Blythe. Don't play ignorant."

"Look, I'm telling you the truth," Artemis said, a note of steel creeping into her tone. "And I'd like to speak to a lawyer before answering any more questions."

"Ah, of course," the male interrogator responded mockingly. "The classic move to avoid giving us any useful information."

"Is it not my right to have legal representation?" Artemis challenged, refusing to be intimidated.

"You came here via a private airport. You're not in the position to be making demands."

"Does Turkey not protect the rights of its suspects?" Artemis demanded.

But the woman ignored this question. The man looked uncomfortable, and Artemis guessed they had moved into the stage where they played fast and loose with the rules.

Still, the woman leaned forward now, studying Artemis' features.

"Tell us something we can use. Why were you at Korkmaz's house?"

Artemis hesitated. She didn't see the harm in providing this information, but her subconscious was desperately trying to decipher why she was in this position to begin with. Who had been tracking her?

They knew about the private plane.

Did they know about Helen?

Certainly not Otto or he would've been in the interrogation room with her...

Unless he was in another room.

The uncomfortable thoughts plagued her, and she huffed in frustration.

"What was that?" the woman said.

"Why not ask Korkmaz about his gambling debt? That's what we were doing—following up on a lead. Forester and I used to work with the FBI."

She decided at this point the truth was perhaps the best avenue. Especially to keep scrutiny off her family.

"We know all about your background," the man said.

"Good. So you know we were just investigating the case."

"You have no jurisdiction in Istanbul," snapped the woman, sounding genuinely irritated.

"I know. We were trying to help a friend."

"So tell me about Mr. Korkmaz," the woman demanded.

"I told you. He had a gambling debt."

"Ms. Artemis," the male interrogator began, his mustache twitching with every syllable. "It appears Mr. Korkmaz had a substantial gambling debt. We already knew this."

Artemis allowed a flicker of surprise to cross her face, feigning innocence. "Oh? So why ask me?"

"Is there anything else we might want to know?"

Artemis's mind was still split, trying to decide how much to give them while searching for any clue that may tell her how much *they* knew already. The less she gave them, the easier it would be to avoid them tracking her movements, potentially reverse engineering them and finding out where her family was shacked up.

But then again, the police were already looking into the honor killing angle.

So Artemis said, "What about Barish Esmer's family? Know about them?"

"Indeed," the female interrogator continued, her piercing eyes boring into Artemis's soul. "And it appears that the Esmer family has been threatening Korkmaz over his daughter."

"Hmm," Artemis replied, noncommittally. "I don't know much about that."

"Perhaps," the male interrogator replied, unconvinced. "But we still need to determine your connection to all of this."

"Of course," she said, maintaining her composure. "But as I've told you before, I won't discuss any details without my lawyer present."

"Fine," the female interrogator snapped, her patience wearing thin. "But there's one thing you can do for us right now. Unlock your phone."

Artemis felt her pulse quicken, the weight of the request settling like lead in her chest. Her phone contained sensitive information that could put her entire family at risk if discovered. Texts to and from her father, from Helen. Tommy getting them a fake ID for Otto, though, they'd used cryptic language. Still... She couldn't—wouldn't—let that happen.

"Absolutely not," Artemis asserted, defiance etched into her pretty features. "As I've stated numerous times, I insist on having a lawyer present."

"Ms. Artemis, refusing to cooperate will only make things worse for you," the male interrogator warned, his voice a low growl.

"Then I suppose we're at an impasse," she replied coolly, her tone unwavering.

The room crackled with tension as the interrogators exchanged glances, their frustration palpable.

"Very well, Ms. Artemis," the female interrogator declared, her piercing eyes narrowing into dangerous slits. "If you continue to withhold information, we have no choice but to consider you an accessory to murder. You'll be spending a long time in prison."

Artemis swallowed hard, feeling the cold fingers of fear tightening around her throat.

"I demand a lawyer!" she reiterated, her voice hoarse with desperation.

"Escort her to a cell," the male interrogator ordered brusquely, his neatly trimmed mustache twitching with annoyance. Two police officers appeared in the doorway, their faces impassive.

As they approached her, Artemis felt her heart pound like a drumbeat in her chest. The cuffs around her wrists clinked loudly as they were unlocked from the table, echoing ominously through the dimly lit room.

Her mind continued to spin.

Thought after thought, move after move.

But all the while, she felt as if her king was exposed, as if her pawn structure had broken down, and as if she were being attacked from every angle.

It reminded her of her last match in the most recent blitz tournament. Her opponent had chased her king from behind his castled wall, but after some time, she'd managed to overwhelm him based on sheer material advantage.

Here, though, she had no advantage.

She was prodded down a dark hall, pushed towards a holding cell.

The scent of urine lingered on the air, covered only vaguely by bleach.

She shivered, inhaling the strange scents.

No sign of Cameron yet, either.

As she was pushed through the gray door, the walls of the prison cell seemed to close in on Artemis, their cold, dark surface reflecting the bleakness of her situation. She sat on the narrow cot, her hands trembling in her lap as she tried to make sense of the chaos that had descended upon her life.

"Think, Artemis, think," she muttered under her breath, her eyes darting around the room, searching for any shred of hope or possibility.

"Damn it," she cursed, feeling the iron cuffs around her wrists chafe against her skin.

Her mind raced through potential strategies, each one more daring and desperate than the last. But with every plan came the sobering realization that failure could mean permanent imprisonment, or worse, harm to her family.

What if she found the real killer though? From inside these walls? She wrinkled her nose, pacing back and forth. If she found the killer, it would clear her name.

"Alright, alright," she whispered, her voice barely audible in the oppressive silence. "Let's start with what we know. Osman Korkmaz's gambling debt, the threats from Barish Esmer's family... There must be a connection there."

She needed to talk with the Esmers, though.

She frowned, remembering a time when Forester had broken her out of prison.

But there was no knight in shining armor coming to her rescue now.

She paused.

How had the Turkish authorities cottoned onto her movements, though? How had they known where to find her?

She considered this a moment, frowning.

They'd seen her at the gambling hall. Then followed her to Korkmaz.

But how would they have known to look for her to begin with?

Unless...

Artemis frowned, her mind whirring.

And then, she froze.

The plane.

The private plane—it was the only explanation. Someone had tracked the plane, tracked their movements, then tipped off the Turkish police.

And as this thought occurred to her, it came with a dawning realization.

"Son of a bitch," she muttered under her breath, and her cool gaze swiveled, finding the camera on the wall outside her bars.

"I know you're watching!" she snapped, staring at the camera. "Let me out. Now! Agent Grant, I'm serious."

There was a pause, as if the whole precinct had gone silent, and then a faint clicking sound at the end of the hall as the door unlocked.

More clicking sounds followed, indicating approaching heels as a tall, sleek figure emerged from behind the door and marched steadily towards Artemis' cell.

CHAPTER 11

SPECIAL AGENT SHAUNA GRANT appeared standing outside Artemis' cell.

Forester's aunt and the taskforce supervisor, she had pale hair which sat in neat curls against her shoulders, framing a face that was better described as handsome rather than beautiful. She had sharp features and eyebrows that looked to be penciled in a permanent frown. Two emerald earrings dangled on either side of her face, swishing briefly until she came to a halt by Artemis' cell.

"Ms. Blythe," Agent Grant said, giving a curt nod of her head.

Even standing there, in a Turkish prison, Agent Grant seemed to command an air of authority.

"You're the one that told them to keep an eye on us," Artemis said softly. "That's why they were on our tail."

"Yes, Ms. Blythe. I like to keep track of my operatives when they make impromptu trips to foreign countries." Grant quirked an eyebrow, peering through the bars. "Quite a predicament you've found yourself in."

Artemis frowned back. "Did you tell them to arrest us?"

Grant ignored the question. She began pacing now, in the dark hall, her heels tapping against the floor in a staccato like a judge's gavel attempting to regain order in a court room.

"Why are you here, Ms. Blythe?" Shauna's eyes peered through the bars like an owl watching a mouse on the forest floor.

Artemis thought of her father, her sister. Her heart skipped a beat. Did Agent Grant know her family was with her?

If she'd been keeping tabs on them, then it was far more than likely.

It had been a mistake to come here, hadn't it?

Artemis shivered. She couldn't say the reason they'd come to Istanbul. Couldn't tell Shauna that she'd wanted a fresh start with her family.

"How did you get the police to arrest us?" Artemis said quietly.

Agent Grant just shook her head. "A favor owed through Interpol. Simple enough. But you haven't answered my question. Why are you in Turkey?"

"Seeing the sights."

"I know you didn't come alone, Ms. Blythe."

Artemis felt her breath catch.

"Yes. I know your father is with you." The FBI supervising agent was still staring through the bars, watchful and attentive.

Artemis felt a cold shiver down her spine.

"So... what are you going to do about it?" she said, her mind racing. With Grant, there was always an angle. Her own nephew was an ex-fighter and self-proclaimed sociopath, and yet she'd kept him on her task force, shielding him from harm.

She had a soft spot for Forester, but the same goodwill didn't extend to Artemis.

"I don't like having my operatives up and leave in the middle of the night. Call me old fashioned."

"We didn't—"

"Save it."

Artemis went quiet.

Grant continued. "Your father and your sister. I have eyes on them currently. They're safe. For now. But the same can't be said for you, Ms. Blythe. And no," she held up a hand as if sensing Artemis was getting ready to speak, "I'm not talking about this... cell... If anything, this is for your own safety."

"What do you mean?"

"I mean... did you know the day after you left Seattle, someone broke into your apartment with the intent to torture and kill you?"

Shauna said it so matter-of-factly that it took Artemis a second to register the words. "Are... what?" She stared.

Grant sniffed. "So you didn't know. We're still trying to track the party responsible. But some chatter we heard between him and his getaway driver was conclusive. He intended you and my nephew extreme harm."

Artemis sat in the cell, reeling.

She had no idea that someone had targeted her and Forester. Who could want them dead? They were just two people trying to get away from their past and start anew. But it seemed that their past had caught up with them. Artemis felt a knot form in her stomach. She needed to protect her family, but how could she do that from inside this cell? "What can I do?" she asked Shauna, her voice barely above a whisper.

Shauna's expression softened slightly. "We need you to come back to the task force, Ms. Blythe. With your skills and expertise, we can catch whoever is after you and Forester. And in exchange, we'll provide you with protection, as well as immunity for any past transgressions."

Artemis stared at Agent Grant.

"Just like that?"

"Mhmm."

"I don't believe you."

Grant shrugged, pursing her lips, and causing wrinkles to stretch the skin like marks in a dry creek bed. "I'm not after your belief, just your agreement."

"Why?" Artemis said, pacing in her cell now. "Why would you go to all this trouble?"

Grant just stared at her, cool, calm, and collected as ever.

"It doesn't make sense," Artemis murmured softly.

Grant leaned against the wall, her eyes never leaving Artemis. The casual posture seemed somehow incongruent with the woman's nature. "Sometimes things don't have to make sense, Ms. Blythe. You're a valuable asset to the task force. And as for your protection, it's our job to keep our operatives safe. It's that simple."

Artemis felt a sense of unease. She knew that with Agent Grant, things were never that simple. "And what about my family?"

"They'll be taken care of. I'll make sure of it."

"Immunity?"

"For your father?"

"For all of us," Artemis said quietly.

"Your brother, you mean?"

Artemis just shrugged. "Blanket immunity. For anything done in the past—all of us." Grant stared at Artemis. "Your father killed multiple women, Artemis. I'm quite interested by this turn of events with him. I hadn't thought you two were close."

"We're not."

"I'm afraid I don't understand."

"Well, that makes two of us."

Grant and Artemis both stared at each other, sizing the other up.

Artemis said, "It's Forester, isn't it?"

Grant blinked.

"You're worried about your nephew. He's the only one that you'd do this for..." Artemis trailed off, then her eyes widened. "Whoever took a shot at us at the apartment... you know who it is, don't you?"

Grant went quiet.

"You do." It wasn't a question.

"Immunity, fine," Grant said simply. "But only in exchange."

"For what?"

"You find the man who's targeting my nephew."

"And me, from what you've said."

"Yes."

"Anything else?"

"Yes," Grant said simply. "You break it off with him."

Artemis blinked. It felt as if she'd just been gut-punched. "I... excuse me?"

Grant sniffed. "I know you two have been sleeping together. I know he's gotten serious about you. I know who you resemble."

"You seem to know a lot."

"I want you to end it. In no uncertain terms. Be harsh so he gets the message."

"And if not?"

"Artemis... your father will spend the rest of his life behind bars," Grant said quietly. She leaned forward, a menace to her tone all of a sudden. "I'll make sure the super-max facility they put him in is air-tight. They'll be no more corrupt wardens to exploit." She held up a finger. "Your brother also will have a special task force assigned to him. Thomas Blythe will join your father—a separate facility of course."

Artemis felt like she was in a nightmare. The thought of ending things with Cameron twisted her stomach into knots.

"I... what if..." She trailed off, stammering.

"It isn't a choice, Artemis. Not really. Find the man after my nephew, break it off with Cameron, and your family and you are pardoned. Simple as that."

"What if I can't do it?" she asked, her voice barely above a whisper.

"Then your father will never see the light of day again."

Artemis felt the tears welling up in her eyes, but she suppressed the emotion, not wanting to give Grant the satisfaction.

She couldn't lose Forester, but she also couldn't let her father spend the rest of his life behind bars. She needed time to think, but she knew that time was a luxury she didn't have.

"I need... I need some time..." she said, her voice shaking.

"I'll give you until tomorrow," Grant said, standing up straight. "But after that, the offer is off the table."

Artemis nodded, feeling like she was in a daze. Grant turned to leave, her motions as brusque as ever.

But as she began to stride away, Artemis said, "Who is it?"

"Excuse me?"

"Who has you this scared?"

Grant turned back, frowning. "Do I look scared to you?"

"No. But you are. You strong arm when you're scared," Artemis said, matter-of-factly. She stared shrewdly at the woman. "You know who's after Cameron, don't you?"

More pursed lips. A hand on a bony hip.

Artemis' mind was racing. "Someone from his past?"

"You have until tomorrow morning."

"Who is it?" Artemis demanded.

"I won't tell you until you agree," Grant replied stiffly.

"I won't know if I can agree unless you tell me."

"If you really cared about my nephew, you'd want to find who was after him. You'd want to end things with him—give him a chance."

For a moment, there was something akin to pleading in Grant's voice. It didn't quite fit the stoic woman's brusque demeanor.

"You really care about him," Artemis said softly.

"He's my nephew."

"I care about him too."

"You don't know him like I do, Ms. Blythe. You two aren't a good fit."

Artemis didn't respond to that. She wasn't sure it was Grant's place to comment on her nephew's romantic chemistry, but she was also very aware of her predicament. Grant held all the cards. Artemis was locked in a Turkish prison, her family was in jeopardy, her relationship was on the line, and not to mention, the murderer of Irem Korkmaz was still at large.

Her mind was reeling now, struggling to piece together her next move.

"Until tomorrow," Grant said softly. "I mean it, Ms. Blythe. I do not make threats lightly. It doesn't please me to do so, but I will end everything you care about if you cross me."

Artemis watched as Grant walked away, her heart heavy with the weight of the ultimatum. She knew that Grant wasn't bluffing; she had seen the woman operate before, and she knew that she was ruthless when it came to protecting her nephew. But the thought of ending things with Cameron was too much to bear. She had never felt this way about anyone before, and the idea of cutting him out of her life was unbearable.

As she sat there, lost in thought, her mind kept returning to the same question: who was after Cameron? She knew that she needed to find out if she was going to have any chance of saving her family. But how? She had no idea where to start, and she knew that time was running out.

She stood up, feeling the weight of the decision bearing down on her. She needed to clear her head and figure out her next move.

Someone had wanted her dead.

Someone was after Forester.

What sort of enemies had Cameron made?

She shivered, feeling a cold chill waft through her cell.

She heard a buzzing sound as the door locked behind Agent Grant at the end of the hall, then once more, Artemis was left in darkness, facing an impossible choice.

CHAPTER 12

ARTEMIS'S EYES FLUTTERED OPEN to the sting of harsh light and the acrid smell of damp concrete. She blinked rapidly, trying to make sense of her surroundings. The cold floor beneath her offered no comfort as she pushed herself up on unsteady arms. Her coal-black hair clung to her face, matted with sweat and grime.

"Where am I?" she muttered under her breath. The dank cell bore no resemblance to the clean lines of her minimalist apartment. She glanced around—there was nothing here but a rusted cot and a grimy toilet in the corner. And suddenly, it all came rushing back.

The events of the previous night—the arrest.

The ultimatum.

Her stomach twisted in knots.

The sudden sound of metal grinding against metal jolted Artemis from her dread. The sound carried with it an ominous weight, like nails scratching down a chalkboard. The cell door groaned open, revealing a quiet security guard standing on the other side. He was a burly man, his face impassive, and he looked at her with a mixture of sleepiness and indifference.

"Get up," the guard ordered in English, his voice barely above a whisper. "You're being released."

"Released?" Artemis echoed, disbelief lacing her tone. She studied the guard's face for any hint of deception but found none. Her heart pounded, a mixture of relief and confusion churning in her chest.

"Come on, then." The guard gestured impatiently, and Artemis struggled to her feet. Her legs wobbled slightly, but she forced herself to stand tall, refusing to let her weakness show.

As they walked through the dimly lit corridor of cells, Artemis couldn't help but wonder what had transpired to secure her release. Had Grant changed her mind?

If so... why?

"Here," the guard said gruffly, stopping in front of a wooden table. "Sign this."

Artemis took the pen he offered with a nod, scribbling her signature on the dotted line without bothering to read the document. She knew better than to question her good fortune—at least for now. As she handed the pen back to the guard, she noticed the tension in his jaw, the way his eyes darted around, never quite settling on hers.

"Thank you," Artemis murmured, her voice barely audible. The guard nodded stiffly, clearly eager to be done with her.

"Go," he said, finally meeting her gaze. "And don't come back."

With a final glance at the man, Artemis stepped out into the sunlight, momentarily blinded by its brilliance. She took a deep breath, filling her lungs with the scent of freedom.

Blinking against the sunlight, Artemis took a few tentative steps forward, trying to regain her balance and think rationally. Being released from jail wasn't a one-man job. Even signing a paper, Artemis felt there should have been more... red-tape? And where was Cameron? She couldn't shake the nagging feeling that something was amiss—that her release from prison had come too easily. She should have known better. In her line of work, she knew not to take anything at face value.

Why would Grant have pulled the strings?

Artemis hadn't agreed to Grant's terms yet.

She tried to push the questions from her mind, focusing on her immediate surroundings. The cacophony of car horns, shouting vendors, and bustling pedestrians filled the air, making it difficult to concentrate. But then she spotted it: a sleek, black sedan idling at the curb nearby, its tinted windows offering no hint of the occupants within.

"Forester," she whispered, her pulse quickening as she recognized the tall, scarred man in the driver's seat. He seemed equally confused by the situation, his dark eyes meeting hers with a mixture of concern and disbelief.

"Artemis!" Forester called out, leaning across the passenger seat to push open the door for her. "What happened? How did you get out?"

"Grant," she whispered tersely to herself, too quiet for Forester to hear, her mind racing as she put the pieces together. Now it made sense. Grant wanted this meeting. Wanted Artemis to speak to Cameron one-on-one.

An icy knot formed in the pit of her stomach, and she shivered despite the sweltering heat.

"Get in the car," Forester urged. "We can't talk here—it's too exposed."

Artemis hesitated, her instincts screaming at her to run as far and as fast as she could. But she knew that wouldn't solve anything; if Grant had gone to such lengths to orchestrate this meeting, there was no escaping her machinations now.

"Okay," she agreed, swallowing hard as she climbed into the passenger seat. It felt like stepping onto a chessboard, the pawns and knights arrayed before her, poised for battle.

But she was already in a losing position.

Forester's disheveled hair framed a face etched with confusion. He glanced at Artemis before settling into the worn seat, and she hesitated for a moment, her heart pounding in her chest. With a deep breath, she climbed into the car, acutely aware of the weight of her decision.

"Are you okay?" Forester asked, concern lacing his tone as he started the engine.

"Fine," Artemis replied tersely, her gaze darting around the car's interior. She couldn't shake the feeling that they were being watched, that Grant's eyes were upon them even now.

As the car pulled away from the curb, Artemis's eyes fell on a small, innocuous object nestled between the seats. It was barely visible beneath the grime and detritus that littered the floor of the vehicle, but it sent tendrils of ice snaking through her veins: a listening device, expertly hidden yet undeniably present.

"Forester," she began, her voice tight with suppressed panic, "we need to talk."

"About what?" he asked, his attention fixed on navigating the chaotic streets of Istanbul.

"Us," she managed, her throat constricting around the word. Her mind raced, searching for a way to communicate the danger they were in without alerting Grant to her discovery.

As the car sped through the bustling streets of Istanbul, Artemis felt her heartbeat pounding in her ears. She remained silent and tense, her eyes darting between the rearview mirror and the hidden listening device that she had spotted earlier. Forester, on the other hand, seemed unaffected by the stress of the situation. He hummed a cheerful tune under his breath, his scarred hands deftly maneuvering the vehicle through the congested traffic.

"Quite a day, huh?" Forester said with a grin, trying to lighten the mood. "I've been working on some new theories about the murder case. I think I might be onto something."

Artemis's stomach churned at the mention of the case. The last thing she wanted was for Forester to delve deeper into it, especially with Grant listening in. She forced a tight-lipped smile and shifted her gaze out the window, avoiding making eye contact with him.

"Let's not talk about that right now," she mumbled, her voice barely audible over the cacophony of honking horns and shouting pedestrians.

"Alright," Forester agreed, his brow furrowed in concern. "But you know you can always talk to me about anything, right? We're a team, Checkers."

Artemis closed her eyes for a moment, feeling the weight of her decision bearing down on her like a crushing burden. The memory of their shared laughter and late-night conversations played through her mind, each treasured moment now tainted with the knowledge of what she must do.

She took a deep breath, steadying herself, and then turned to face Forester. "Actually, there is something I need to tell you."

Forester glanced over at her, a playful smile tugging at the corners of his mouth. "Oh, really? What's up?"

Artemis hesitated, the words catching in her throat. She swallowed hard and forced herself to speak, her voice barely more than a whisper. "I think we need to break up."

"Break up?" Forester echoed, his eyes widening in shock. The car swerved slightly, as he momentarily lost focus on the road. "What do you mean?"

"Please," Artemis pleaded, her hands gripping the edges of her seat, "just trust me on this."

Forester's confusion was evident in the furrow of his brow, but he didn't press further. Instead, he gripped the steering wheel tighter, knuckles turning white, and stared straight ahead.

The silence between them was suffocating. Artemis felt it tighten around her chest, constricting her breath. She stared out of the car window, trying to focus on the bustling cityscape outside, but her mind kept racing back to the decision she had made.

"Artemis," Forester said gently, the playfulness that had once leaped from his voice now replaced with a muted concern. "You need to tell me why."

She clenched her fists in her lap, nails digging into her palms. The pain grounded her, providing a brief respite from the whirlwind of emotions threatening to consume her. "I can't," she whispered. "You're better off not knowing."

"Better off?" His voice cracked, and Artemis winced at the raw vulnerability she heard there. This wasn't how she wanted things to be, but she couldn't see any other way.

"Forester, please." She glanced over at him, her heart breaking at the sight of his furrowed brow and downcast eyes. "You have to trust me."

His grip on the steering wheel tightened further, knuckles turning an even whiter shade of pale. "Trust you?" he asked, his voice barely audible over the hum of the engine. "How can I trust you when you won't confide in me?"

He wasn't getting angry, wasn't stretching himself to his full height, shoulders square like when he faced down a group of attackers.

He just looked lost and confused... and very tired.

Artemis squeezed her eyes shut, fighting back tears. She knew the cost of telling Forester the truth—it would entangle him deeper in the web of deceit that she so desperately wanted to escape. And yet, it pained her to see him like this, his trust eroding beneath the weight of her silence.

"Forester..." she began hesitantly, struggling to find the words that could explain her decision without revealing too much. "Sometimes, the hardest thing we have to do is let go of the people we love the most. I'm trying to protect you—and my family. That's all you need to know."

"Protect us?" Forester's eyes met hers, desperation etched into the lines of his face. "From what, Artemis?"

She knew what she was to him. Knew, in a way, she'd replaced his lost love. The woman who'd been murdered. But she had hoped, and believed, they'd developed their own relationship. And now...

She was dashing all of it against the rocks.

"From everything," she whispered, her voice trembling with emotion. "From the darkness that follows me wherever I go."

For a moment, neither of them spoke. The only sound in the car was the steady rhythm of tires on pavement, carrying them further away from the life they had once shared together.

"Artemis," Forester said at last, his voice low and heavy with sadness. "I would face anything for you. You don't have to do this alone."

"But I do," she replied softly, staring straight ahead as tears streamed down her cheeks. "It's the only way to keep you safe."

And with that, she knew that there was no turning back. In her heart, she understood that the road ahead would be long and lonely, but it was a path she had chosen—for herself, for Forester, and for her family.

As the car rumbled forward, the distance between Artemis and Forester seemed to grow by the second. She could feel his eyes on her—pleading, searching for an answer that she couldn't give him. Her heart clenched with a sorrow so profound it threatened to engulf her, but she steeled herself and faced him, determination etched into every line of her delicate features.

The listening device threatened her.

Grant would make her life hell. her father, her brother... her sister.

Or they could all be pardoned. Forester would be safe.

And Artemis just had to bite back the words. She couldn't tell Cameron. No. Grant would know she'd been crossed.

"I need to get out!" Artemis said suddenly.

"Wait, hang on. Art, hang on!"

But she was shaking her head, her eyes blurry. But she couldn't stay in the car. it was too painful.

She shot a vengeful look towards the listening device and resisted the urge to mutter hope you're happy.

She reached for the door handle, her hand trembling as she forced herself to speak. "I'm sorry, Forester."

"Artemis, don't go!" he called out, like a child lost in the darkness. But she couldn't stay—not if it meant his life was at risk.

She flung open the door, and he screeched to a halt, his protective instinct overriding his desire to keep her near.

With one last glance at the man who had come to mean everything to her, Artemis stepped out of the car and onto the sun-baked pavement. The door slammed shut, severing their connection and leaving her feeling more alone than she'd ever felt before.

As she hastened away, she could still see Forester's bewildered expression through the rear window, his eyes silently begging for answers she could never give him. And as she turned her back on him, her heart shattered into a thousand pieces, each one a testament to the love they once shared and the sacrifices she would make to keep him safe.

She would have to speak to Grant. Soon.

She massaged at her wrists, though the cuffs were long gone.

She thought of Izel...

Irem's killer was still out there.

The person who Grant claimed had threatened Forester was still out there.

Artemis shook her head, muttering darkly to herself.

Grant would come in contact soon enough. Artemis knew that much now. She'd been foolish to think she could get out from under the woman's thumb.

But in the meantime...

She picked up her pace, moving hastily through the city. She didn't know where she was going—but she spotted a tall skyscraper in the distance that looked familiar.

She used this as a guiding signpost, heading steadily towards it.

She needed to find her family. To get her father and sister to safety.

As the thought lanced through her, she let out a desperate breath and waved at an approaching, yellow taxi, flagging it down.

CHAPTER 13

THE SOLDIER'S EYES BORED into the manifest before him, the dim lamplight casting a yellowish hue on the paper. His fingers traced over the list of names as if he could summon Artemis from the ink itself. His heart quickened when he found her name—Artemis Blythe, seat 23A. He committed it to memory.

The faintest hint of a smile tugged at the corner of his mouth.

"Reginald," the soldier barked into the phone, knowing that his butler would answer promptly. "I need you to make some arrangements."

"Of course, sir," Reginald replied in his usual calm tone, betraying not a single hint of the urgency that bubbled beneath the surface. "What do you require?"

"Book two tickets on flight TK1829. We're taking an unexpected trip to Istanbul."

"Very well, sir," Reginald said. "May I inquire as to the nature of this trip?"

"Artemis and Cameron are within reach," the soldier responded, his voice cold and resolute. "I won't let them slip away again."

"Understood, sir. I will ensure everything is prepared for your departure." Reginald's unwavering loyalty comforted the soldier in a way few other things could.

As the soldier hung up the phone, his thoughts turned once more to Artemis. Despite her plain appearance, with her coal-black hair and simple clothes devoid of makeup or piercings, he knew all too well the cunning that lay beneath her pretty features. She was a chess master, always plotting her next move, manipulating others like pieces on a board.

***

The sun dipped below the horizon, casting a warm golden glow over the airfield. The soldier and the butler strode purposefully across the tarmac, their eyes fixed on the sleek private plane that awaited them. Its engines hummed softly in the background, like a predatory animal lying in wait.

"Sir," Reginald began, his voice a quiet murmur in the soldier's ear, "I've taken care of all the necessary preparations. We should have no trouble reaching Istanbul."

"Good." The soldier's voice was terse, his mind already working through the myriad possibilities that lay ahead. "We can't afford any delays. Not this time."

As they neared the gleaming aircraft, the soldier couldn't help but admire its streamlined beauty. It was a fitting instrument for a man who had dedicated his life to the pursuit of excellence.

Once inside, the soldier paused to survey his surroundings. The interior of the plane was just as luxurious as the exterior promised, with plush leather seats and polished wood paneling. But the soldier paid little heed to these trappings of wealth; his mind was consumed by thoughts of revenge.

"Is everything to your satisfaction, sir?" Reginald asked, his voice betraying only the faintest hint of concern.

"Quite so, Reginald," the soldier replied, forcing a tight smile. "Now, let's get this show on the road, shall we?"

"Of course, sir." With a nod, Reginald turned to relay the soldier's command to the pilot.

As the plane began to taxi down the runway, the soldier allowed himself a brief moment of reflection.

The smell of polished leather and gasoline mingled in the air as the soldier settled into his seat, feeling the firm cushioning envelop him. The engine's hum grew louder, steadily drowning out the cacophony of the bustling airfield outside. He fastened the seatbelt around his waist, the metal buckle cold against his fingers.

"Would you like a drink before we take off, sir?" Reginald asked, suddenly appearing at the soldier's side.

"Whiskey. Neat," the soldier replied, his voice steady and focused.

"Very well, sir." Reginald nodded and moved toward the small bar located near the front of the plane.

As the soldier stared out the window, he watched the flurry of activity on the tarmac. Ground crew members scurried about, fueling planes and loading luggage, their faces determined and resolute. He clenched his fist, his prosthetic arm creaking slightly under the pressure.

He had killed a woman who'd resembled Artemis before...

And he'd gotten into a plane much like this one to do it.

He smiled.

"Your whiskey, sir," Reginald announced, returning with a glass filled with amber liquid. The soldier accepted the drink, nodding his gratitude.

"Reginald, have you ever been to Istanbul?" the soldier asked, taking a sip of the whiskey. It burned pleasantly as it slid down his throat, igniting a fire in his belly that matched the intensity of his thoughts.

"Once, many years ago, sir. It's a beautiful city, rich with history and intrigue," Reginald replied, an almost wistful look crossing his face. "But I imagine our focus will be elsewhere during this trip."

"Indeed," the soldier agreed, his gaze never leaving the window. "We have a mission to complete."

"Of course, sir."

"I'll need you at your best, Regi. There are things I may ask of you. Things you won't understand at the time." He placed his hand on the butler's arm, and Reginald flinched. "I can trust you to obey, yes?" he stared into Regi's soul.

The man swallowed and bobbed his head. "Y-yes, sir."

As the plane's engines reached a crescendo, the ground crew dispersed, leaving only the sleek machine and its occupants on the tarmac. The runway stretched out before them like a challenge, daring the soldier to chase down his quarry.

"Let's go," he murmured, his eyes narrowing as the plane began to accelerate. He could feel the vibrations in his seat, the power of the aircraft channeled through his very bones.

"Checkmate," the soldier whispered, gripping the armrests tightly as the plane charged forward.

He nodded, feeling his muscles tense as his hands tightened on the glass of amber liquid.

He'd decided that he'd make Forester watch this time.

It would be more fun that way.

CHAPTER 14

ARTEMIS PUSHED OPEN THE door to her new apartment, weary and fearful.

"Dad? Helen!"

No answer.

She looked around the unfurnished space, her heart in her throat.

"Dad?" she called out. "Helen?" her voice louder.

Still no response.

A chill ran down her spine as she looked around the empty space. The only things in the room were a few cardboard boxes, some of their belongings from home, scattered on the floor. She stepped carefully over them and made her way to the kitchen.

The light was dim but she could still make out the outline of a small table and two chairs tucked into one corner. On it was a half-empty glass of water and a copy of her father's favorite book, The Count of Monte Cristo, which he must have brought with him when they moved here. But there was no sign of her father or sister.

Artemis' fear deepened as she wandered back into the living room, taking everything in. She walked towards an open window, pulling aside the curtains to peer outside at the quiet street below; still no sign of them. Her stomach began to knot as she thought about Agent Grant and her threats—had she taken them away?

She quickly made her way to each bedroom, searching frantically for any clues as to what might have happened to her family—nothing seemed out of place. As panic set in, Artemis rushed around the apartment looking for anything that would help her find them—but all she found were more unanswered questions and growing dread that they may never be seen again.

Finally exhausted from searching every corner of the apartment for any sign of her father or sister, Artemis slumped onto Helen's bed and let out a long breath.

And that's when she saw it.

A single piece of paper.

It fluttered and twirled, having fallen out from under the pillow. Artemis caught the piece of paper before it hit the ground.

Forester would've been proud of her reaction time...

But thoughts of Forester only further soured her mood, so she quickly returned her attention to the piece of paper.

A sheet of chess annotation.

Her heart skipped.

She swallowed.

This was the sort of thing that her sister might use to communicate. She'd done so in the past. At the time, though, Helen had been battling her own demons. Artemis felt her heart skip a beat at the thought of her sister in Agent Grant's custody.

Would Helen's darker inclinations return?

"Shit," Artemis said, her eyes scanning the chess annotation, trying desperately to make sense of it.

Was it in code?

She recognized the match, though, it took a moment.

One of theirs.

In fact... it was a match they'd played yesterday in the small chess club inside the gated community.

She quickly pushed the piece of paper into her pocket and hastened back out the door.

She took the marble steps three at a time as she hurried down the bottom floor, pushed out onto the marble walkway, and circled the railing surrounding the pool as she moved towards the single-story building which housed the pool changing rooms on one side, and the chess club on the other.

She spotted a few players on the patio, engaged in their own games.

But no sign of Helen or her father.

"Come on," she whispered under her breath.

She reached the chess club, pushing the door open swiftly. All the while, she felt a cold shiver down her spine. Inside, more players were engrossed in more games. Players of all ages gathered around the roll-up boards. But there was still no sign of her father nor of Helen.

Artemis was beginning to panic.

Her gaze was drawn to the door in the back of the club, which led to the office where she'd spotted Izel crying the night before.

Without hesitation, Artemis made her way to the door, her heart pounding in her chest. She pushed it open slowly and peered inside. The room was small and cramped, with a single desk in the center and a few chairs scattered around the walls. A faint smell of cigarette smoke lingered in the air.

And there, sitting behind the desk, was Helen.

"Artemis!" Helen said, happily. "We've been waiting for you!"

"Shut the door behind you," her father called from where he was standing by a window, peering out into the street. "The car is still out there."

"You're here!" Artemis exclaimed.

"Yes," their father said ."Now, please, shut the door."

"What car?" Artemis said, frowning, her mind still reeling as it competed for both relief and curiosity.

"SUV. Federal plates—embassy," her father said. He glanced back at her. "You don't know anything about it, do you?"

Helen cut him off, though, saying, "I knew you'd know where to find us."

"Yeah, well, you left me that clue. Nice thinking... Did Izel let you back here?"

Helen nodded. "She said you were a friend of hers. Recognized me from our game yesterday."

Artemis glanced around the small office space, and she spotted a light glowing under the door at the back of the room. She heard the sound of a sink running.

Artemis pointed at the door and quirked an eyebrow. "She back there?" Artemis said in a faint whisper.

Helen nodded once, moving so that she sat on the front of the desk, her tanned legs swinging over the side.

Their father was still by the window, frowning in the direction of the parked car.

"Americans, definitely Americans."

Artemis wasn't sure how he'd determined this by the way a car was idling, but she knew better than to question the seasoned mentalist's intuition.

She approached the window, peering out as well at the vehicle lingering outside their gated community.

"I had a meeting with a federal agent last night," she said quietly.

179

"We know," Helen said. "He's really handsome."

A lance of guilt shot through her. "No. Not Forester."

Her father and Helen both looked sharply at her.

"Agent Grant. She... she knows about you, Dad. She knows you're here."

A faint hush had fallen over the room now, and Artemis could hear the ticking of the clock on the wall. Their father's expression had hardened, his eyes narrowing with suspicion and calculation.

"How much does she know?" he asked, his voice low and dangerous.

Artemis swallowed hard, feeling the weight of her father's gaze on her. "Enough to threaten you. Tommy."

"Just me?" his eyes darted to his older daughter.

"Just you," Artemis shot back.

To his credit, her father looked somewhat relieved by this news. Then he stood up, his eyes flashing with anger. "It's time to move," he said, his voice cold and decisive.

"Not possible," Artemis said. "She's been watching the airports. That's how she knew we'd left."

"Train then," her father said. "Or boat."

Artemis hesitated. "I... I have a deal on the table. Immunity. For all of us."

"All?" Helen said, eyes widening.

"A sort of blank check, for any past crimes," Artemis said.

Everyone shared a sidelong look. The implications of this weren't lost on any of them. The sound of running water from the bathroom continued unabated.

"What do you have to do in exchange for this immunity?" her father said slowly.

Artemis crossed her arms, glancing through the window at the parked car across the street.

"Find out who took a shot at Agent Forester."

"Someone took a shot at him?" Helen said, sounding concerned.

"Apparently."

"Grant told you this?"

"Yeah."

"Where is the big guy?" her father said.

Artemis winced. She felt as if her insides were being twisted. She didn't want to talk about Cameron. She couldn't help but wonder where he was, and how he was feeling.

He didn't have emotions like most people... but where she was concerned, things were different.

Artemis shivered, letting out a faint sigh.

"I see," her father said before she'd even spoken. "And this was Grant's idea too? To break up with him?"

"Yes."

"Oh, Art, I'm sorry," Helen said, hurrying forward and wrapping her arms around her younger sister. "You didn't need to do that. Not for me!"

But Artemis just hugged Helen back without speaking for a moment.

She knew that she had made the right decision, no matter how much it hurt. She had to protect her family, and that included Cameron.

Finally, Artemis pulled away from Helen's embrace and took a deep breath. "We need to figure out our next move," she said, her voice firm. "I'll take the deal, but we need to be careful. We can't trust anyone."

Her father nodded in agreement. "Agreed. We'll have to lay low for a while, but we'll come up with a plan."

As they spoke, the sound of the running water from the bathroom suddenly changed.

It wasn't the sound of water pouring into a sink now but, rather, water spilling over porcelain and slapping against the floor.

Artemis frowned, and all three of her family members glanced toward the bathroom door as one as if their instincts were in perfect synchronization.

"Izel?" Artemis called out. "Is everything okay in there?"

When there was no answer, Artemis took a step forward, a feeling of unease settling in her stomach. She reached for the doorknob, turning it slowly. The door creaked as it opened, and Artemis stepped into the bathroom.

The small room was filled with steam, and the floor was slick with water. Artemis's eyes widened as she saw Izel slumped against the wall, her head tilted to one side. The water had overflowed from the bathtub and was now pooling around her. Artemis had thought the sink was running. Who took a bath with three strangers just outside the door?

But this was a fleeting thought. Izel was still clothed but soaked.

"Izel!" Artemis rushed over, her heart pounding in her chest. She grabbed Izel's shoulders, shaking her gently. "Wake up, Izel!"

But Izel remained unresponsive, her eyes closed and her breathing shallow. Drenched in the bathwater, there was a bag lying next to her, floating on the water. It took Artemis only a few seconds to piece together what had happened.

Izel had tried to suffocate herself.

Artemis's mind raced as she tried to figure out what to do. She couldn't call for help, not with the federal agents outside. And she didn't know enough about medicine to help Izel herself.

She glanced up at her father and Helen, who had followed her into the bathroom. "We need to get her out of here," Artemis said urgently. "We can't leave her like this."

Her father nodded, his face grim. "I'll carry her out. Helen, grab some towels and meet us out front."

As her father lifted Izel into his arms, Artemis felt a sense of relief wash over her. At least they were doing something, taking action.

Her mind was still spinning though.

Why had Izel tried to kill herself?

The young woman's head lolled to the side as Otto Blythe gently carried her through the door.

The man they'd accused of being the Ghost Killer, of targeting young women, was now attempting to save the life of one.

But just then, there was a shout.

A man was standing in the doorway. It took Artemis a second to recognize Izel's father, the coach who'd been so kind to Helen and Artemis the previous day.

He was staring into the room, just through the doorway.

His deep, brown eyes were the size of saucers.

"Izel!" he shouted, his voice rising in fear. He rushed towards them in a lunging motion, arms outstretched to grab his daughter's form.

Artemis stepped back as Izel's father reached them, his eyes wild with panic and despair. He looked at Otto, then at Artemis and her family, his gaze scanning each of their faces as if searching for answers.

"What happened?" he demanded, his voice shaking. "What did you do to her?"

Artemis's father stepped forward, his tone calm and measured. "We didn't do anything to her," he said. "We found her like this. We're trying to help her."

Izel's father's eyes flicked to the bag that was still floating in the water, visible through the open door where steam gushed into the office, and his face contorted with anger. "What's that?" he growled, pointing at the bag.

"It's hers," Artemis said, her voice barely above a whisper. "She was trying to hurt herself."

Izel's father let out a cry of anguish, sinking to his knees beside his daughter's limp form. He buried his face in his hands, his broad shoulders shaking with sobs.

Artemis felt a lump form in her throat as she watched him. "Let us help you," she said gently. "We'll take her to the hospital."

Izel's father looked up at her, his eyes red and swollen. "No! No, you stay away from my family!" He was panicked, lashing out.

But he snatched his daughter's form from Otto, and spun around, breaking into a sprint, shouting as he did, "Yardim et! Lutfen! Yardim et!"

Artemis stared after his retreating form, feeling her own stomach sink.

"What the hell just happened," Otto said.

But Artemis had turned on her heel now.

It couldn't be a coincidence. Two young women, best friends. One of them murdered by drowning. The other tried to take her own life in a bathtub.

What was going on here?

Artemis raced into the bathroom, looking around desperately. There was a window in the back. Ajar.

Had someone slipped through?

She approached the window, frowning.

It was locked from the inside.

No... The floor was slick under her feet. She turned, examining the bathroom... There was no other way in.

Izel had done this to herself.

But why?

Why now?

"Did she seem suicidal when you talked to her?" Artemis said, glancing back at Helen.

187

Before her sister could reply, their father said, "We need to leave, girls. The feds are coming."

Helen just shook her head. "She seemed normal. Sad... but normal."

Artemis frowned. She knew that most people couldn't really read the emotions of others, but if Helen was telling the truth... normal... Then something was very abnormal about what had just transpired in the bathroom.

It was connected to Irem. It had to be.

Artemis spotted a phone sitting by the sink, and her eyes widened. She reached out, swiping the phone's face with trembling fingers. The screen was locked, but new messages bubbled at the bottom, the notifications lighting up the device.

She tried to open the phone, but the passcode was four digits. The probability of randomly guessing it was low. Artemis's mind was racing, figuring out what to do next.

She needed to know what was on that phone.

"Come on, Artemis," her father said urgently, his hand on her shoulder. "We have to go now."

Artemis hesitated for a moment, then made a decision. She grabbed the phone and turned to follow her family out of the bathroom.

They had to get out of there before the feds arrived. But Artemis knew that she couldn't let this go. She had to find out what was going on with Izel and Irem.

"I hope she's going to be okay," Helen said softly.

Artemis glanced over.

For a brief, horrible moment, she wondered if Helen had somehow been involved in this.

But no.

No, this was Helen. NOT the Ghost Killer.

Artemis knew the difference.

Her sister hadn't shown any episodes for quite some time.

No. She refused to believe it.

They also had the money, now, to hire the best doctors in the world. She just had to get that immunity, and they just had to make it to the next day.

But for now...

189

Grant hadn't gotten in touch yet.

Which meant there was a window of time, a sliver of daylight in which Artemis was still free.

Her eyes narrowed as her family hastened out the back exit, under a glowing, red sign. She needed to unlock this phone, to figure out who had been texting Izel. And if they'd also texted Irem.

Something was going on here...

Something that made her skin crawl, and she still didn't know what.

CHAPTER 15

SHE'D TOLD HER FAMILY to stay away, but she'd decided to return to the lion's den. It had seemed like the only way to get the phone unlocked, and time was ticking.

Artemis stood outside the Turkish police precinct, her hair fluttering in the cool breeze. Her nerves were evident as she paced back and forth, trying to keep her mind focused on the task at hand. The unfamiliar surroundings weighed heavily on her already troubled mind; Istanbul was a world away from the predictable life she had left behind.

Her eyes scanned the horizon, taking in the breathtaking features of the city. The skyline shimmered like a mirage, an enchanting blend of history and modernity. Ornate minarets rose in harmony with sleek glass towers, while the domes of ancient mosques nestled amidst the sprawling metropolis. Istanbul's unique architectural landmarks—the Hagia Sophia and the Blue Mosque—loomed majestically against the backdrop of the Bosphorus Strait, serving as silent witnesses to centuries of change.

As she gazed across the cityscape, Artemis found her thoughts drifting toward the challenges that lay ahead. Her mind raced with the intricate strategies she'd need to employ, each move and countermove unfolding like a perfectly choreographed dance.

"Focus," she muttered under her breath, reminding herself that she couldn't afford any missteps. There were lives hanging in the balance—not just her own, but also those of Izel and Artemis's family.

Cameron's life...

A sudden gust of wind whipped her hair across her face, snapping her back to reality. Artemis took a deep breath, willing her racing mind to slow down and concentrate on the next move. She'd been pacing outside the precinct for nearly a half hour now.

Grant would've known she was there.

Was the woman simply making her wait?

Artemis frowned towards the closed doors of the precinct.

But even as this thought troubled her, and while she did everything she could to push aside thoughts of Forester, the door to the Turkish police precinct swung open, and Artemis caught sight of Agent Grant striding toward her. The agent's white hair gleamed under the sun like a beacon in contrast to her stern features and no-nonsense demeanor.

"Ms. Blythe," Grant said, standing tall and poised before her. Her gaze was sharp and scrutinizing as she regarded the younger woman.

"Agent Grant," Artemis replied, summoning a quiet confidence. She met the agent's eyes, knowing full well that hesitation would only invite suspicion. "I need your help."

"With what?" Grant inquired, folding her arms across her chest.

"I need a phone unlocked," Artemis admitted, her words measured and careful. She didn't wait for a response, but kept speaking, marching steadily on. "It belongs to Izel, a girl who tried to commit suicide after her friend Irem was murdered. I believe there's a connection between their actions and something more sinister at play."

Grant raised an eyebrow, her interest piqued despite her skepticism. "And how does this concern you, exactly?"

"Two lives were nearly lost," Artemis countered, her voice steady. She knew the gravity of the situation warranted her involvement. Plus, she was now on the hook with Grant. This was very likely her last autonomous act for some time.

"Your sense of justice is admirable, but this isn't my jurisdiction," Grant reminded her, her tone firm yet not unkind. "What makes you think I can help you?"

"Because you have access to resources I don't," Artemis replied, unwavering. She understood the delicate balance she needed to maintain—pressing her case without overstepping her bounds. "And because I did what you asked."

"I heard," Grant said simply.

Artemis had spotted the listening device but didn't mention it. With Grant, it was often best to play cards close to the vest.

Grant's steely eyes bored into Artemis, her voice cold and unyielding. "I don't have the authority to unlock that phone for you. Jurisdictional limitations apply, and frankly, this case isn't a priority for us. I trust you haven't forgotten the *other* half of our arrangement?"

Artemis clenched her fists, nails digging into her palms. She knew she was treading on thin ice, but she couldn't let Izel down. Not after what had happened to Irem.

"Please, Agent Grant," she implored, her voice shaking with the intensity of her emotions. "Izel needs our help—she could be in grave danger. And if there's even the slightest chance that unlocking this phone could save her life, then we have to take it."

For a moment, it seemed as though Grant might relent, but then she shook her head, her expression resolute. "My hands are tied."

"Look, I did what you asked—!"

"Artemis, you know I've already bent the rules for you once," Grant said, her voice tightening. "I can't keep making exceptions. Besides... we have other priorities." She quirked an eyebrow. "Breaking up with Cameron was a necessary step, but hardly worthy of immunity for your father and brother."

"For my whole family," Artemis said.

Grant looked sharply at her, and Artemis looked away, not wanting to reveal anything in her countenance.

"Quite so..." Grant said carefully. "But regardless..." she trailed off. "You have another case. An urgent one."

Artemis nodded, hesitant. "Whoever took a shot at Cameron is stateside, yes?" "Yes."

"And so if they are really determined to get him, they'll come here, won't they?"

Grant just nodded.

"So what if we solved this case for the Turkish police?" Artemis pressed. "They'd owe us one. We could leverage the favor into an APB at mass transit and transportation. Otherwise, we'd be flying blind."

Grant stared at Artemis, and Artemis returned the expression.

"That's a neat little bow you've tied on it, now, isn't it?" Grant said speculatively. "You'll solve this case for the Turkish police, and you hope that in return they'll keep an eye out for anyone crossing into the country on flight manifests."

Artemis bobbed her head once.

Grant sighed, massaging her nose. "You really do have a knack for this, you know. It's a pity about your background. You might have made a good supervising agent one day."

Artemis didn't find this to be a compliment, but she didn't say so.

Grant was now striding back and forth, shaking her head from side to side.

"Fine," she said, at last, turning back towards Artemis. "I'll see what I can do about the phone. But if there's nothing on it, or it doesn't lead anywhere, that's it. No more favors."

Artemis breathed a sigh of relief, her heart racing with renewed hope. "Thank you, Agent Grant. I won't let you down."

"You better not," Grant warned, her tone stern. "You have twenty-four hours."

Artemis blinked.

"I mean it. One day," Grant said, holding up a finger as cold and unwavering as a rod of ice. "And then we're done. We focus full attention on the attempt on Forester's life."

"Where is Cameron?" Artemis said.

"That doesn't concern you anymore, does it? He's going to be assigned to a separate task force."

Artemis felt a pang in her stomach and bit back a response. She held her tongue channeling the frustration into a brusque nod. Inwardly, she was seething, but she knew better than to attack from a position of weakness. She had to wait, to bide her time.

She had strings to pull now that Grant likely knew about but didn't anticipate.

Artemis was locked in a chess match, and this time... she needed the immunity for her family.

After that?

Then she could make her move.

"When..." she said slowly, "When can my family sign their papers?"

"Immunity? Not yet. Not until you find this man who's after my nephew."

"So you know he's a man?"

"Yes."

"What else do you know?"

"Time will tell. But I have my suspicions."

Artemis frowned at Grant, and the severe woman glowered back.

"Now. Phone," Grant said, extending her fingers and waiting expectantly.

Artemis bit her lip, but then sighed, extending the device towards the agent.

Grant took the phone from Artemis' hand, studying it intently. "I'll make some inquiries," she said, turning to leave. "But don't get your hopes up. This could be a dead end."

Grant strode back into the precinct and gestured for Artemis to follow. Inside, she extended a perfectly manicured hand to a room just off to the side of the sliding glass doors, calling over her shoulder, "Wait in there. Don't leave. Keep the door shut."

Artemis hastened after the supervising agent into the foreign police station, her head ducked, trying to avoid the prying eyes of the local police.

Following Grant's pointed finger, Artemis stepped into the interrogation room and closed the door behind her. The air felt heavy, oppressive, as if it had witnessed a thousand confessions and still held on to the secrets they whispered. She tried to shake off the feeling, but isolation gnawed at her like a persistent ache.

She paced the length of the room, each step echoing against the cold, concrete floor. Her mind raced with calculations, probabilities, and contingencies. If she could just unlock that phone, she might find the key to unraveling the mystery of Izel's connection to her friend's death.

Her fingers traced the edge of the metal table, tapping out an impatient rhythm. In her head, she reviewed the conversation with Agent Grant, dissecting every word, every nuance. Had she made the right choice? Artemis was used to relying on her intellect and intuition to guide her, but now, more than ever, she needed them both to stay sharp.

She kept thinking of Forester.

How many times had the two of them been in a room like this together?

But once those immunity papers were signed...

Things would change.

Artemis knew she was playing a dangerous game. One didn't cross Agent Shauna Grant without repercussions, but she was in too deep now.

Besides...

If someone really was after Cameron, she wanted to find out who it was just as much as Grant did. But another part of her wondered if all of this was just a ploy to attempt to drag Artemis back stateside.

As these thoughts whirled through her mind, she could feel the passage of time flash by. Each of her footsteps tapping rhythmically against the floor was like the ticking of a second hand. The passage of time all seemed to blur together, until a knock on the door startled her, halting her pacing in its tracks.

The door swung open to reveal a technician, his eyes hidden behind thick glasses. He carried a smartphone in one hand, the screen now unlocked and displaying a series of text messages.

"Here you go," he said, handing over the device with a nod.

"That was quick."

"Was easy. Jailbroken phone." He shrugged. "Good luck."

"Thanks," Artemis replied, taking the phone with an eager grip. The tech gave her a final glance before disappearing back into the precinct.

"Alright, let's see what we've got," she murmured, scrolling through the messages sent to Izel. As she read, her brow furrowed in confusion.

There was only one thread, which had occurred during the suicide attempt: a series of pictures sent from an unknown number.

Artemis's spine stiffened, an uncomfortable dread chilling her extremities.

The screen was filled with pictures of Izel's father, the chess coach. Each image seemed to capture him at his most vulnerable—asleep, unaware, walking to a tea house. Drinking on a porch.

"Who would send these?" Artemis wondered aloud.

Her gaze shifted to the bottom of the text, where a number caught her attention.

5000.

She stared at the number.

5000. Just like the debt owed by Osman Korkmaz, the murder victim's father.

5000. But this time, under the chess coach's image. Why? Was he also in the pocket of the bookie? Or was something else going on here?

Artemis was frowning at the screen. For a moment, she considered going to the hospital and speaking to the chess coach... but no. No this wasn't something that had been sent to him. It had been sent to Izel.

Why? Why was someone threatening her? Was that what this was? A threat? Izel had tried to kill herself after receiving these photos... why?

Artemis knew she needed to find out the answers to these questions and fast. She quickly copied over the pictures and screen-grabs of the phone's display before shutting off the device.

As she made her way back out into the precinct's main floor, she could feel her heart pounding in her chest. She had a hunch that this was just the tip of the iceberg, and she needed to act fast before someone else got hurt.

But as she stepped out into the bright sunlight of the Istanbul streets, she couldn't shake the feeling that she was being watched.

Artemis paused, scanning the crowds for any sign of danger, but everything seemed normal. She took a deep breath, pulled her jacket tighter around her, and started walking.

Twenty-four hours to solve the case.

Twenty-four hours to figure out who had sent the pictures.

And now, as she marched forward, she had a pretty good idea where to start.

CHAPTER 16

THE AIR INSIDE THE dimly lit Istanbul bar was thick with smoke and the scent of alcohol, as an eclectic mix of patrons filled the room. Laughter and lively conversations in a multitude of languages echoed around the dark wood-paneled walls, punctuated occasionally by the sharp clink of glasses, as old friends and new acquaintances toasted to their good fortune or drowned their sorrows.

In the shadows, the soldier stood inconspicuously, his eyes scanning the bustling crowd. His heart pounded with anticipation, and he could feel the adrenaline surging through his veins.

"Is that him?" he wondered, the weight of his concealed knife pressing against his hip. He had been waiting for this moment for what felt like an eternity.

His butler had tracked the lumbering galoot to this watering hole on the far-flung side of the world.

As if on cue, Forester emerged from the throng, his tall frame towering above most of the other patrons. The disheveled state of his hair and clothing seemed to match the scar that marred the palm of his hand—a detail the soldier had committed to memory. The agent's voice rose above the din, his words heated as he argued with a Turkish man whose face grew redder by the second.

"Seninle işim bitmedi!" the Turkish man spat, his anger evident in every syllable.

"Look, pal," Forester retorted, trying to keep his own emotions in check. "I don't have time for your games right now."

The soldier watched intently, his senses heightened by the conflict unfolding before him. He knew that this could be the chance he had been waiting for, the opportunity to strike while Forester was preoccupied. But something held him back. It couldn't be easy for Cameron—no. No, he had to suffer.

The soldier watched as Forester's patience wore thin; the alcohol coursing through his veins fueled his agitation. He stumbled forward, pushing the Turkish man with more force than necessary. "I said, back off!" he slurred, his voice raised in anger.

The bar's murmur fell to a hush as the tension in the air grew palpable. In a fluid motion, three of the Turkish man's friends stepped forward, their faces twisted into hostile scowls.

"Ozur dile," one demanded, his voice icy and unwavering.

"Is this really necessary?" Forester asked, his words slurred but his tone dripping with condescension. "I don't think any of us want to make a scene."

"Aptal erif," replied the third man, cracking his knuckles menacingly. The room held its breath, the clinking of glasses replaced by an eerie silence.

"Alright, alright," Forester sighed, raising his hands in mock surrender. "You win. I'll apologize, but only if your friend here admits he started it."

The Turkish man who had been shoved narrowed his eyes in defiance.

"Fine," Forester said, a feral glint in his eye. "Just remember, you asked for it."

As if on cue, the three men lunged forward, their fists raised and aiming straight for Forester. His inebriation caused him to sway on unsteady legs, but he quickly regained his footing. The alcohol coursing through his veins only added fuel to his resolve.

With lightning-fast reflexes, Forester ducked under the first attacker's punch, his hand darting out to land a precise strike on the man's solar plexus. The attacker gasped for breath, doubling over in pain.

The second attacker charged, attempting to tackle Forester to the ground. But even in his intoxicated state, Forester's combat training was etched deep into his muscle memory. He sidestepped the man, who stumbled awkwardly past him. Seizing the opportunity, Forester grabbed the man's arm and twisted it hard, forcing him to the floor with a howl of agony.

"Ol artik!" the Turkish man snarled, launching himself at Forester with a flurry of wild punches.

Forester dodged the blows with ease. He waited for an opening, then struck like a cobra—fast and deadly. His fist connected with the man's jaw, snapping his head back with a sickening crunch.

"Three," Forester said aloud, panting as he surveyed the aftermath of the brawl. The three men lay defeated and groaning on the floor, victims of their own bravado.

Hidden in the shadows, the soldier observed Forester with a mixture of contempt and admiration. He had never seen anyone fight with such ferocity and skill while also being drunk. The glint of the hidden knife in his hand caught a stray beam of dim light as he tightened his grip on it.

He remained in the shadows, wondering what might happen were he to reveal his face to Cameron.

But no...

Slow. He reminded himself.

He wanted to take this slow.

Forester panted as he surveyed the aftermath of the brawl. The three men moaned on the floor.

Forester's still the same, the soldier thought, watching the man closely.

"Is that all you've got?" Forester taunted the room, swaying slightly on unsteady legs. His disheveled hair clung to his sweat-drenched face, and his breaths were heavy and uneven. The adrenaline pumping through his veins fought against the alcohol in his system, leaving him disoriented and vulnerable.

"Enough!" the bartender shouted in English, his voice cutting through the cacophony of excited chatter and clinking glasses. "Get out! All of you!"

"Fine by me," Forester replied, wiping blood from his split lip. As he stumbled towards the exit, a few patrons moved aside, giving him a wide berth. The soldier tensed, ready to spring into action if necessary. At this moment, however, his target was no t hreat.

"Keep your distance," the soldier reminded himself, maintaining a secure vantage point as he continued to watch Forester. The bar's dim lighting created pockets of shadow perfect for remaining unseen. His thoughts raced, considering the implications of what he had just witnessed.

"Forester's dangerous even when drunk," he thought, conflicted. But he wasn't afraid of the ex-fighter.

He'd hurt Cameron before, and he'd do it permanently this time.

The door swung closed behind Forester, and the soldier paused for a moment before following him out into the night. He couldn't afford to lose his target, but he also needed to be cautious. The streets of Istanbul were alive with the hum of a thousand conversations and the distant call of muezzins from their minarets.

As Forester stumbled through the vibrant city, the soldier shadowed him, his grip on the hidden knife ever tightening.

Forester moved in the cool night air, his breaths ragged and uneven. The soldier's gaze followed him intently, never straying from the staggering figure that was now his prey.

He trailed Forester through the winding streets, his footsteps as silent as a cat stalking it's quarry. His senses heightened to their maximum, detecting the faintest sounds and fluctuations in the air around him.

"Hey!" a voice shouted, breaking the soldier's train of thought. He glanced over to see a street vendor hawking his wares, seemingly oblivious to the life-and-death struggle about to unfold. The soldier gritted his teeth and returned his focus to Forester.

But Cameron was gone.

The soldier frowned, glancing one way, then the other.

Where had he disappeared too?

His gaze scanned the Turkish streets, and his heart skipped a beat.

Shit. He'd been distracted. Where the hell was the fighter?

The soldier cursed under his breath, scanning the alleyways and side streets for any sign of Forester. He couldn't afford to lose his target, not now when he was so close.

Suddenly, a figure stumbled out from behind a nearby dumpster, and the soldier tensed, ready to strike. But as the figure stumbled into the light, he realized it was just a homeless man, drunkenly shuffling along with a bottle in his hand. The soldier sighed in frustration, his adrenaline still pumping from the excitement of the chase.

He continued to search for Forester, his eyes darting back and forth as he scanned the streets for any sign of the fighter. But the city was vast, and the night was dark. It seemed as though Forester had disappeared into thin air.

Taking a deep breath, the soldier set off into the night once again, his senses on high alert.

It couldn't be that hard to find a giant, drunken American in the heart of Turkey.

No... no, he had to keep attentive.

His prosthetic arm brushed against his pant leg as he moved forward, and his gaze swept the path ahead of him, searching.

The tell-tale signs of an Istanbul night stood out:

the smells of the street food, the sounds of music and laughter spilling out from the smoky bars, and the cool breeze that carried with it a hint of salt from the nearby sea.

The soldier's gaze flitted over the crowds, but Forester was nowhere to be seen. He cursed under his breath, frustration building inside him.

Suddenly, he heard a faint sound that made his heart skip a beat. It was the sound of a struggle, coming from a narrow alleyway just ahead. Without hesitation, he sprinted towards the noise.

He rounded the corner and then pulled up short.

Cameron was trying to push a dumpster.

The soldier just stared, quizzical.

The struggle wasn't that of man against man, but man against metal.

Forester grunted as he shoved the dumpster towards a fire escape ladder.

The soldier watched, still unsure of whether to reveal himself or not. He could see that Forester was struggling, his drunken state making it even more difficult for him to move the heavy object. The soldier's grip on his knife tightened, but he made no move to approach Forester just yet.

As if sensing someone watching him, Forester turned his head, his bleary eyes meeting those of the soldier. His expression turned from confusion to recognition as he realized who was standing before him.

"You," he slurred, taking a tentative step forward. "What do you want? I killed you! You're dead..."

The soldier realized Cameron wasn't really seeing him. He was seeing a ghost. Drunk as he was, he likely wouldn't even remember.

The soldier remained silent, his gaze locked onto Forester's. He could see the confusion and fear in the fighter's eyes, but he had no intention of speaking just yet.

Forester took another step forward, and the soldier tensed, ready to strike if necessary. But then, to his surprise, Forester slumped against the dumpster, his eyes closing as he slid to the ground.

The soldier hesitated for a moment before approaching him cautiously. He knelt down beside Forester, checking his pulse to make sure he was still alive. He could feel the rapid beat of the fighter's heart.

The soldier sighed, feeling a strange mix of relief and disappointment. He had hoped for a bit more of a fight.

He stood up, glancing around the alleyway to make sure that no one else was around. Satisfied that they were alone, he slipped his knife back into its sheath and pulled out his phone.

He realized his one good hand was trembling in excitement.

He allowed himself a small smile of anticipation.

Then, phone in hand, he spoke. "Bring the car around," he said. "To this address. I have him. Hurry."

CHAPTER 17

ARTEMIS GLANCED AT HER wristwatch, the second hand ticking away in a cruel reminder that time was relentlessly slipping through her fingers. She exhaled sharply, trying to quell the rising anxiety within her chest. Twenty-four hours to clear a murder case.

The deadline loomed mercilessly, and there was no room for error. Her mind raced with contingencies, each possibility analyzed and dissected with the precision of a blitz match. She had to solve this case before it was too late.

As she approached the gambling hall, its dimly lit entrance seemed to beckon her into a den of vice and deception. Faint yellow light spilled out onto the pavement from the half-open door, casting eerie shadows on the cracked concrete. Muffled voices emanated from within, a cacophony of laughter and despair intermingling in the night air. It was the sound of desperation, the sound of dreams being shattered and fortunes lost.

Standing on either side of the entrance were two burly guards, their imposing figures shrouded in darkness. Their eyes scanned the street with steely precision, vigilant for any signs of trouble. Artemis knew they were protecting more than just the patrons inside; they were guarding a web of secrets that stretched far beyond the confines of the gambling hall.

The weight of the ticking clock pressed down on Artemis like an invisible hand, each second slipping through her fingers like sand. Time was running out, and she knew that every moment counted. As she approached the gambling hall's entrance, her steps were measured, her focus unwavering.

A dim light barely illuminated the façade of the building, casting eerie shadows that seemed to dance and flicker with the muffled voices emanating from within.

Another figure stepped from inside the recesses of the door, and now three burly guards stood watch, their expressions grim.

Much closer now, she realized their bruised faces and torn clothing bore testament to their recent encounter with Forester.

"Evening," Artemis said, keeping the stammer from her voice and addressing the guards with a cool confidence as she drew closer. She was lying with her tone, and it took everything in her to prevent her knees from knocking together. The men eyed her warily, their hands flexing at their sides.

"İşte o!" a guard muttered under his breath in Turkish, his eyes narrowing with suspicion.

"Merak etme," a second replied, equally low, also speaking in Turkish. "Eğer sorun çıkarırsa, onunla başa çıkarız."

Artemis kept her gaze steady on the first guard who had recognized her. She knew that they would be cautious of her presence, but that could also work to her advantage. "I'm here on business," she replied simply, her voice unyielding.

The third guard, the one who'd been inside, stepped forward. His arm was in a sling, and Artemis winced as she studied Forester's expert work.

The man was glaring at her, contempt in his eyes. Clearly, he recognized her.

"Business, huh?" The guard sneered, cracking his knuckles threateningly. He spoke with an American accent—not Turkish then. Just an opportunist. "Well, we don't take kindly to snoops around here, especially ones who stick their noses where they don't belong."

She decided not to point out the redundancy of this statement.

"Believe me," Artemis replied, her mind racing as she calculated her next move, "this is one situation where I'd rather not be sticking my nose. However, circumstances demand it."

The guard growled, stepping forward with his comrades to block her way.

"İyi şanslar," the second guard said, smirking. She wasn't sure if he could understand any of the exchange but decided not to press the question.

"Enough with the threats," Artemis said coolly, guessing at the content of the latest entreaty as she stared unflinchingly into the eyes of the guard who had recognized her. "I'm here to deliver something Mehmet will be very interested in."

She reached into her jacket pocket, her movements slow and deliberate so as not to alarm the guards. She produced a thick envelope, filled with cash. She'd pulled it from the ATM before arriving. "Mehmet's money," she announced, holding it up for them to see. "I know his reputation, and I know he's been waiting for this. Are you going to keep him waiting even longer?"

The guards exchanged wary glances, their conversation switching back to Turkish as they muttered among themselves. Their suspicion was palpable, but Artemis could also sense an undercurrent of fear threading through their words—fear of what would happen if they denied their boss the money he was owed.

"Çok akıllı değil" one of them grumbled, shooting her a distrustful look.

"İş arkadaşı" another chimed in, as the trio seemed to reach a reluctant consensus.

"Fine," the third guard finally spat. He jerked his head toward the entrance, signaling for her to follow. "You're coming with us, but don't think we'll hesitate to put you down if you try anything."

"My only concern right now is getting this situation resolved," Artemis replied, her voice steady as she mentally cataloged every detail around her. They grabbed her roughly by the arm, escorting her through the dimly lit doorway and into the heart of Mehmet's lair.

Her arm ached under the pressure, but she knew better than to protest.

They were dragging her deeper into their lair.

"Keep your eyes forward," one of the guards growled, giving her arm a painful squeeze. She winced but refused to let him see any sign of fear.

As Artemis passed through the heavy, velvet curtain separating the outside world from the gambling hall, she was immediately struck by the opulence that enveloped her. The room stretched out before her like a lavish banquet, with gilded mirrors lining the walls and sparkling chandeliers casting a warm glow over the polished mahogany tables.

"Good God," she muttered under her breath, taking in the sheer extravagance of the scene. "It's like Versailles in here."

"Keep moving," one of the guards snapped, shoving her roughly forward.

Though the hall's décor exuded wealth and luxury, Artemis couldn't help but notice the darker elements lurking just beneath the surface. The patrons themselves, for one, seemed a motley assortment of unsavory characters—men with greasy hair and weathered faces, women draped in furs and jewels that spoke of ill-gotten gains.

"Watch yourself, girl," the guard warned her, as they navigated their way through the bustling hall. "These people aren't your friends."

"Neither are you," Artemis shot back, scanning her surroundings with the keen eye of a chess master, always looking for her next move. She could feel the tension simmering beneath the veneer of respectability, the unspoken threat of violence hanging heavy in the air. It was a game, she knew, where the players were as much a part of the stakes as the money being won and lost on the tables.

As they moved deeper into the labyrinthine space, Artemis observed the various games in progress, noticing the fervent desperation in the eyes of some players, while others seemed to thrive on the chaos and excitement. Roulette wheels spun wildly, and cards were dealt with practiced precision, each new hand carrying the potential to make or break fortunes.

"Your boss, Mehmet, he enjoys this madness?" she asked the guard, her concerns piqued despite the danger she found herself in.

"He profits from it," came the terse reply. "Now be quiet."

Artemis filed away this information, knowing that every detail she learned about Mehmet and his operations could prove invaluable in her quest to outwit him. She held tightly onto her determination like a lifeline threading through the chaos of the gambling hall guiding her ever closer to the heart of the criminal enterprise she suspected had been the cause of Irem's death and Izel's suicide attempt.

She wasn't sure yet.

That's why she'd come here. A fishing expedition.

Dangerous, yes, but she didn't have the luxury of caution.

The guard pushed open a nondescript door, revealing a dimly lit room that appeared to be a stark contrast to the opulence of the gambling hall. Artemis took a moment to assess her surroundings: the walls were bare, save for a single painting of a serene landscape, and the only furniture was an unassuming wooden desk, behind which sat Mehmet.

It looked different during the light of day, the sun still entering the room through the stained glass windows behind the master of the gambling hall.

He wasn't the bumbling, nervous fool his front-of-the-house bookie had played the last time they'd come. He was in control, his strained pride stiffening his back. Artemis briefly wondered about the fate of the underling she and Forester had intimidated on their last visit.

"Sit," he commanded, his voice devoid of any warmth. His appearance was deceptively ordinary—a middle-aged man with graying hair and a tired expression. Yet, his eyes betrayed a cunning and ruthlessness that had earned him a fearsome reputation in the criminal underworld.

She'd learned far, far more about him now in the drive over. It was amazing the things one could find on the wide open internet.

"Thank you," Artemis replied, taking a seat in the chair opposite Mehmet. She felt the familiar sensation of adrenaline coursing through her veins, heightening her senses and sharpening her mind. She breathed in slowly, steeling herself for the confrontation ahead.

"Let's not waste time," she said calmly, looking directly into Mehmet's cold gaze. "You know why I'm here."

He leaned back in his chair. "I don't think I do."

She frowned, crossing her arms. "I want to pay Osman's debt."

He blinked at her, adjusting his spectacles. His brown suit sleeves brushed against the side of his neatly groomed face.

"I see," he said. "And why would you want to do that?"

"Does it matter?"

"My business. It matters."

Artemis could feel the gaze of the guards Forester had roughed up. They were still behind her, lingering in the doorway, and likely waiting for the slightest excuse to give her a beating.

She returned her attention to the bookie.

He sat primly on the edge of the table, his legs crossed, his hands folded in his lap.

"It's in exchange for a favor," she said simply.

"What favor?"

"Leave Izel alone."

He blinked. "Who?"

He had barely hesitated. He was quick. Very quick, but there had been a brief moment of recognition.

Why should he know Izel's name?

But of course, she knew why.

He was lying.

Playing her.

But she could see through it now, and she wasn't going to take the bait again.

She said, "I know you killed Irem."

"I did not." Even quicker this time.

"Fine. You had her killed."

He just watched her, his eyes not quite like a snake as she'd first thought. More like a shark. A predator that was constantly on the move.

"I had nothing to do with her death," he said evenly. "And I have no idea who this Izel person is."

Artemis knew he was lying, but she also knew that she needed to tread carefully. She couldn't afford to give him any reason to turn on her, not when she was so close to uncovering the truth about Irem's death.

She took a deep breath and tried a different approach. "I can help you," she said, leaning forward so that she was eye-level with Mehmet. "I know things that could be of use to you."

He raised an eyebrow. "Such as?"

"Information. Tips. Connections."

"Go on."

Artemis could feel the tension in the room building, the guards behind her shifting their weight ever so slightly as they tightened their grip on their weapons.

"Mehmet, you're a smart man," she said, her voice low and persuasive. "You know that in this business, knowledge is power. And I have a lot of knowledge that could be of use to you."

Mehmet considered her for a moment, his eyes darting over her face. "You can't imagine me that stupid, no? What is it you want? Why are you here? Why are you stalling?" He frowned at her for a moment longer, then clicked his fingers.

"Check her for a wire!" he snapped.

Two of the guards rushed forward. One more hesitant than the other, likely taking a second longer to translate the command.

Artemis felt her stomach plummet. She tried to rip her hand from the grasping grip of one of the guards, but he held tight. The other tugged at her shirt, lifting it to reveal her pale stomach.

Mehmet leaned back in his chair, watching with a cold detachment as the guards searched Artemis. His eyes flicked over her body, taking in every detail with a calculating gaze. Finally satisfied, he gave a curt nod and the guards released her.

"You're clean," he stated, his voice void of any emotion. "But I still don't trust you."

Artemis gritted her teeth, her hands clenching into fists at her sides.

"I understand your caution," she said, her voice low and even. She tried to ignore the men who were still so close, who'd almost enjoyed the opportunity to manhandle her. "All I'm asking in return is for you to leave Izel alone. Let her go, and I'll give you everything you need to take your operation to the next level."

Mehmet leaned forward, his eyes glinting with a dangerous light. "How long have you been in Istanbul? A few days? A week? You come into my house; assault my guards; disrespect *me*. And now you want to tell me how to conduct my own business? Why? Why should I believe you? And even if you speak the truth, why should I cooperate?"

"Because I have something you want," Artemis replied, holding his gaze. "Forget information. I have cash. Lots of it. This is just a taste."

She extended the envelope she'd been holding.

The guard with the sling snatched it from her, holding it up for Mehmet to examine.

Mehmet took the envelope from the guard and opened it. His eyes widened as he counted the stack of hundred-dollar bills inside.

"Where did you get this?" he demanded, his voice laced with suspicion.

"It doesn't matter," Artemis replied, her heart beating wildly in her chest. "All that matters is that it's yours, in exchange for leaving Izel alone."

Mehmet considered her for a moment, his eyes flicking over her face. Then, he stood up from his chair and walked over to her.

He stood so close she could smell his cologne, a musky scent that made her feel nauseous.

"And tell me," he said, his voice low and dangerous. "Now that you've come and freely handed me this tribute, what other leverage do you have?"

And in a flash, a gun appeared in his hand, pulled from behind his back.

He aimed the gun at her forehead, his lips curving into a snarl.

"You shouldn't have come here."

CHAPTER 18

THE COLD METAL OF the gun barrel pressed against Artemis's forehead sent a shiver down her spine, its deadly promise echoing through her very core. She stared at the weapon, her heart pounding in her chest like a caged animal trying to break free. The room seemed to shrink around her, as if the walls were closing in, suffocating her. It was a dangerous game she had chosen to play, and now she stood face to face with the ultimate consequence.

Mehmet sat perched on the back rest of a chair now, one leg crossed over the other, a predatory gleam in his eyes even as his outstretched hand kept the gun against her. He exuded an air of power and control that seemed to fill the room, casting a shadow over Artemis. Despite the imminent danger, she couldn't tear her gaze away from him. He looked relaxed, almost amused by the situation, his fingers on his free hand tapping rhythmically against the tabletop.

"Quite the predicament you find yourself in, eh?" Mehmet said with a smirk, his voice dripping with menace.

Artemis swallowed hard yet refused to let the fear consume her. She focused on the man before her, taking in every detail—the way his eyes flickered between her and the gun, the subtle curl of his lip as he spoke, and the slight tilt of his head as he studied her.

A sharp pain in her arm drew Artemis's attention away from Mehmet for a moment. She glanced over her shoulder and saw the thug who had accompanied her, his injured arm wrapped in a makeshift sling, the other hand gripping her arm tightly. His breath was hot on her neck, and she could feel the malice radiating from him. The danger he posed was palpable.

"Should I take care of her?" he said, sounding excited.

Mehmet didn't answer him directly, but instead addressed Artemis.

"Such a pretty little thing you are," Mehmet drawled, eyes raking over her as if she were nothing more than a piece of meat. "It's almost a shame, really. A young woman like yourself should be enjoying life, not meddling in things that don't concern her."

Artemis gritted her teeth but refused to let her fear show. "You're wrong, Mehmet. This does concern me."

"Ah," he said, leaning forward slightly, a glint of amusement in his eyes. "But is it worth your life?"

"Maybe it is," she replied, locking her gaze onto his. Artemis knew she needed to hold onto whatever control she could in this situation. If she fell apart now, there would be no coming back from it.

"Very brave," he commented, smirking at her defiance. "Or very foolish. Time will tell."

"Listen," Artemis said, her voice steady despite the cold sweat trickling down her back. "I have the money you're after."

Mehmet's arrogant smirk faltered for a moment, replaced by a quizzical expression that seemed out of place on his cruel features. His thick brows furrowed, and he tilted his head to the side like a curious bird. "Yes... yes, you did come with money. A strange choice. It has me curious... You are very curious, aren't you?"

Artemis clenched her fists, nails digging crescents into her palms. She drew strength from the pain, using it to anchor herself in the present moment.

"Osman's debt," she said, soldiering on and trying to keep her voice from trembling. "I know what he owes you, and I can pay it off—every last lira." She held her breath, watching Mehmet's reaction closely.

The gangster regarded her with undisguised suspicion, his eyes narrowing as he tried to decipher her intentions. He leaned back, drumming his fingers against the table, creating a staccato rhythm that echoed through the room like the ticking of a clock.

"Very interesting," he mused, his voice dripping with sarcasm. "But we've been over this. Why should I not just take the money, and deal with you? Especially after you come in here, slinging round accusations."

Artemis narrowed her eyes, studying Mehmet's every twitch and shift as he leaned forward.

"Look, I know you killed Irem," Artemis said, her voice steady despite the cold dread creeping through her chest. "And now you're threatening Izel's father. But I'm here to end this, right now."

Mehmet's lips curled into a sardonic smile, one eyebrow arching incredulously. "You're quite the detective, aren't you?" he mused, tapping his temple with the gun in a mocking salute. "But tell me, how exactly do you plan on ending anything?"

His words hung in the air like a challenge, but Artemis refused to falter. She could feel the thug behind her shifting uneasily, no doubt itching to wrap his injured arm around her throat. The pressure was mounting, but she knew that if she showed any sign of weakness, it would only embolden them.

"Osman's debt is cleared," she stated firmly. "But you will leave Izel and her family alone, and we'll never speak of this again."

Mehmet leaned back in his chair, a cruel glint in his eyes as he considered her proposal. The silence stretched between them, suffocating in its intensity.

"Is that so?" he finally drawled, shifting the gun and aiming it squarely between her eyes. "And what makes you think you have any say in the matter?"

Artemis stared him down, her heart hammering in her chest as she weighed the risks of revealing her hand. She knew there was a chance he'd call her bluff, but she had no other option—not if she wanted to save Izel and her family.

"I work with the FBI," she said simply. "American. My supervising agent is named Shauna Grant. She's in Istanbul right now. If you kill me, you'll draw the attention of not only Americans but also Interpol and likely your own government. It's one thing to kill teenage girls, but it's another to kill an FBI agent."

She stared at him, determination in her gaze.

It was a bold play.

But the truth often took courage.

Besides, it was a calculated risk.

Men like Mehmet thrived like cockroaches, in the dark, in shadow. He thrived hidden from view.

She hoped that the threat of international attention would be enough to make him back down. But Mehmet's expression remained unreadable. He studied her for a moment longer before finally breaking into a grin.

"You know, I enjoy a woman with some backbone," he said, his eyes glinting with something that made Artemis's skin crawl.

"Double," Mehmet drawled, leaning back in his chair and crossing his legs. "I want double the amount. Call it a fee for the pain you have caused me and my men."

Artemis's heart clenched at his words, her chest tightening with anxiety. She hadn't anticipated this demand from him, but she knew that showing any signs of hesitation would only weaken her position.

"Fine," she replied, her voice steady despite the swirling emotions within her. "If that's what it takes, I'll make sure you get double the amount."

"Are you so eager to save them?" Mehmet asked, a cruel smile playing on his lips. His eyes were locked onto hers as if he could see right through her facade of confidence.

"Ah, Miss Artemis," Mehmet sighed theatrically, shaking his head. He twirled the gun and began tapping it against his chin, a dangerous glint in his eyes. "You are such an interesting woman. So full of surprises."

"Enough with the games," Artemis demanded, her patience wearing thin. "Do we have a deal or not?"

"What makes you think I had anything to do with Irem?"

"I looked you up," she said simply. "It's how you handle business. You go after family members. It was the way Irem died. Drowned like that. You were sending a message—it reminded me of a cartel killing."

He just watched her, unmoving.

"You threatened Osman. That was why he looked so guilt-stricken when we talked to him. He wasn't shocked, just sad. He knew his daughter was in danger. But he didn't know she'd gone to see you. She'd put herself in harm's way by reveal-

235

ing who she was to you. It immediately made her a target. You had her followed, didn't you?"

Mehmet still said nothing.

But Artemis nodded once. "You did. And that was it. You gave the order." She trailed off. "And that still wasn't enough, was it? Izel was next. Irem's best friend. You assumed that by threatening Izel's father, you'd be threatening someone Osman cared about. But the two of them weren't friends. Only their daughters."

"You seem to know a lot," he whispered.

"I've been looking into you," she said simply. "And I know men like you. It was the purse."

"The what?"

"The purse," she said simply, shrugging. "At first, we'd thought it was stolen by the killer. But later we found out someone came along later and took it. Which meant the real killer left the purse at the crime scene."

He stared at her as if trying to read her thoughts.

She said, "You didn't know Izel would kill herself. You were just trying to scare her to get your money. So here I am. With your money."

He let out a long, deep exhale.

"I see," he said simply.

She straightened now, staring at his gun. And then she said, "Read the back of that envelope."

He frowned, flipped the envelope over, and leaned in to where the cramped writing had been hastily scrawled.

Artemis knew she was right.

She also knew that she needed this man to pay.

As he was distracted, looking at the scrawled message on the back of the envelope, he looked up. "Triple the pay?" he said, sounding impressed.

And then the window shattered.

Two gunshots.

They echoed loudly.

The bullets hit one after the other. Artemis gasped and stumbled back, toppling from the chair. She let out a wheezing sound, clutching at her chest as crimson pooled down her fingers, over her heart.

She blinked, staring and gaping up at Mehmet. "I... I..." she trailed off, her voice going quiet.

He was staring down at her, his eyes bugged out. For a moment, it was as if he couldn't process what he was seeing, but then he turned, and yelled, "What the hell was that!"

Artemis lay gasping on the ground. More gunshots echoed through the window. And then, far closer than they should've been, the sound of sirens.

Crimson continued to pool through her fingers, soaking her shirt, and spreading across the ground.

CHAPTER 19

THE DEAFENING ROAR OF gunshots ripped through the air, shattering Mehmet's thoughts and plunging him into a whirlwind of chaos.

Panic bubbled in his chest as he instinctively dove for cover behind the heavy mahogany table in the center of the room, his fingers tightening around the cold steel of his own weapon. He nearly lost his glasses, and his hand shot up, returning them from where they attempted to slip off his nose.

"Get down!" someone screamed, their voice barely audible above the relentless barrage of gunfire. Mehmet's heart raced, slamming against his ribcage as adrenaline coursed through his veins. He knew he needed to act fast if he was going to survive this onslaught.

"Who the hell is doing this?" he muttered under his breath, his eyes darting around the room in search of the attackers. The thick, acrid smell of gunpowder hung in the air, mingling with the scent of fear.

The deafening echo of gunshots hung in the air like a death knell as Mehmet pressed himself against the floor, his heart pounding like a furious drumbeat. His hands clenched around the cold steel of his own weapon, ready to fire at a moment's notice. The acrid smell of smoke filled his nostrils, an unwelcome reminder of just how close he was dancing with the reaper.

"Artemis," he whispered, cursing her name under his breath. He dared to peek out from behind the overturned table and immediately wished he hadn't. There she lay, her lifeless body sprawled across the floor, eerily still amidst the cacophony. Her coal-black hair fanned out around her head, framing her pretty features like a macabre halo. But it was her eyes that haunted him the most; one blue, one hazel, they stared sightlessly upward, forever frozen in a moment of shock.

"Damn you," he muttered. This was her fault. He didn't know how, or why. But he knew she was to blame.

"Boss, we've got to move!" a guard shouted in Turkish over the din, dragging Mehmet back to the present. Mehmet knew the man was right. They were sitting ducks here, and every second they hesitated brought them closer to joining Artemis in whatever afterlife awaited them.

"Right." Mehmet gritted his teeth, forcing down the bile that threatened to rise in his throat. "Let's go."

With a surge of adrenaline, Mehmet pushed himself up from the ground and fired off a round in the direction of the shattered windows.

The gunshots were coming from the abandoned building across the street. He couldn't see the shooters though. The window behind him exploded in a shower of glass, shards raining down like deadly confetti, as another barrage of bullets tore through the room.

"Cover me!" he shouted, sprinting across the room and ducking behind a pillar as more shots rang out. His mind raced, trying to formulate a plan amidst the chaos—but all he could think about were Artemis's mismatched eyes, glaring accusingly at him from beyond the grave.

"Boss, we need to find cover!" the guard with the sling yelled again, his voice barely audible over the relentless gunfire. He was right; they couldn't hope to hold their ground here.

"Follow me," Mehmet ordered, his voice hoarse.

Mehmet's heart pounded in his chest, a jackhammer against his ribcage, as the adrenaline coursed through his veins. He peered around the pillar, eyes scanning the room for any sign of an exit route. Every nerve twitched with the insistent need to move, to escape the death trap he suddenly found himself in.

The sirens were getting closer.

"Shit. Who called the police?" his guard said where he stood at his elbow, also taking cover behind the pillar.

"Artemis was an FBI informant," Mehmet muttered under his breath, his voice barely audible amidst the gunfire. "Interpol, the FBI... they're going to be all over this." His mind raced, the implications of Artemis's death crashing down upon him like an avalanche. There was no way out of this, not without leaving a trail of bodies behind—and even then, would that be enough?

She'd brought the cops to his doorstep. Someone had called them ahead of time.

What the hell was going on?

Desperation clawed at his throat, urging him to flee, but he forced himself to think rationally. Someone had set this up, orchestrated the entire scene to have Artemis killed on his doorstep. That same someone wanted him dead, too—or worse, captured and imprisoned for the rest of his life.

"Cover my retreat!" he ordered, gritting his teeth as he prepared to make his move. A split second before he dashed from his cover, the distant wail of sirens was joined by another, closer sound of approaching sirens. They were all around him, the sounds growing louder with each passing moment. Time was running out; the police would be swarming the building soon.

"Got it, Boss," the guard replied, unloading a torrent of bullets in the direction of their unseen enemy to create a brief window of opportunity. Mehmet seized it, sprinting across the floor and hurdling over Artemis's lifeless body as he made his way to the nearest exit.

Whoever did this... they'd pay, Mehmet promised himself, a furious fire burning in the pit of his stomach. But first, he needed to survive—and that meant getting out of this hellish nightmare in one piece.

As the sirens grew louder and the acrid scent of gunpowder filled his nostrils, he knew he couldn't waste any more time.

He moved down the service hall, which led away from the bullet-riddled room.

Ahead, the EXIT sign glowed in faint neon.

His eyes locked onto the two guards blocking the path to the back door. They looked confused, both of them trying to shove a trolley of poker chips through as if the plastic pieces would have any value after tonight.

"Get out of the way!" Mehmet screamed.

But the two guards didn't hear or were too busy to notice.

"I said get out of the way!" he screamed again.

One flinched, but only glanced back, and then gave an extra shove on the cart full of useless plastic.

Mehmet had enough.

He aimed his weapon, squeezing the trigger twice in rapid succession. Two sharp cracks echoed through the chaos, and the guards crumpled to the floor, blood seeping from their wounds.

"Sorry, boys," Mehmet muttered as he stepped over their lifeless bodies.

With adrenaline coursing through his veins, he sprinted towards the back door. Each pounding step felt painfully slow, like running through quicksand.

As he reached the back entrance, his heart sank.

"Hands up!" voices shouted in Turkish. "Freeze! Freeze! Get on the ground. Drop the gun!" A deluge of commands flooded him.

He froze in place, staring at the scene before him, visible through the wide-open double doors leading to the parking lot. A squad of police officers stood waiting, guns drawn and shouts ringing through the air. The cold realization that he'd been cornered settled like a weight on his shoulders.

"Hands up! Don't move!" one officer commanded, his voice strained with urgency.

The sirens wailed closer, blending with the cacophony of shouts and gunfire, creating a symphony of chaos.

Mehmet's eyes darted between the officers, assessing his options. Sweat trickled down his temple, mingling with the blood from a superficial wound caused by the shattered glass.

"Drop your weapon!" an officer barked, his voice cutting through Mehmet's thoughts like a knife.

"Last chance!" the officer yelled.

"Damn it all," Mehmet muttered under his breath, knowing that fighting back would only lead to his own demise.

At least five weapons bristled towards him, like the quills of a porcupine.

With a heavy sigh, he let the cold steel of the gun slip from his grasp, clattering against the pavement. He raised his hands above his head, defeat weighing heavily on his shoulders.

"Get on the ground! Now!" another officer ordered.

Mehmet obeyed, dropping to his knees before lowering himself onto his stomach. The rough concrete dug into his skin as he stretched his arms out, feeling the icy handcuffs close around his wrists.

As the police officers encircled him, Mehmet surrendered to the realization that he was well and truly trapped. The adrenaline coursing through his veins began to recede, replaced by a cold dread that settled in the pit of his stomach. He couldn't help but think of Artemis Blythe, her mismatched eyes staring accusingly at him as if goading him to take one last desperate swing at fate.

"Curse you," he whispered, his voice barely audible over the screaming of sirens.

"Quiet!" snapped a Turkish cop, grabbing Mehmet's arm and yanking him to his feet. His other hand clamped around the cuffs on Mehmet's wrists, tightening their grip and causing him to wince in pain.

"Move!" the officer barked, pushing him forward.

Mehmet stumbled, struggling to maintain his dignity amidst the flurry of activity outside his building. As they passed the front entrance, he caught sight of a body being hastily dragged out, covered in a blood-soaked sheet. It took all his self-control not to react, biting the inside of his cheek until he tasted iron.

Artemis Blythe lay lifeless on the cot, being pushed towards a waiting ambulance.

"Keep moving!" the cop growled, giving him another shove.

He allowed the officer to guide him towards the waiting police car, its blue and red lights flashing ominously in the darkness. Despite his predicament, he couldn't help but hold onto a sliver of hope—that somehow, Artemis Blythe wouldn't recover. But those shots had hit center mass...

Her death gave him some small satisfaction.

Because one way or another, she'd brought this to his doorstep.

"Get in," the cop ordered, opening the door to the back seat.

Mehmet hesitated for a moment, casting one last glance at the chaos unfolding around him. Then, with a final whispered curse for the woman with the mismatched eyes, he climbed into the vehicle.

The door slammed, and he peered through the glass.

His eyes lingered on a gurney being wheeled towards the waiting ambulance.

"Is she dead?" Mehmet asked hoarsely, unable to tear his gaze away from the woman who had ruined everything.

Now, he'd be prosecuted. If she was tied to the FBI, and if she'd died on his doorstep, everyone—all the enemies he'd ever made—would attempt to use this to their advantage.

"Shut up," the cop snapped, but Mehmet barely heard him. All his attention was focused on the paramedic leaning over Artemis, pressing two fingers against her throat in search of a pulse that would never come. The medic exchanged a grim look with his colleague before shaking his head and pulling a white sheet over her face. Satisfaction surged through Mehmet—she was gone. But the taste of victory was bitter, tainted with the knowledge that he was still trapped in the back of the car.

But Artemis Blythe was dead...

And so was everything he'd ever built.

He felt a tear form in his eye as he stared in the direction of the old warehouse he'd used for the gambling hall.

He'd built it all with his own hands...

But Irem Korkmaz... a step too far. He'd wanted the money from her father... he'd thought it would work...

But now...

He sighed, closing his eyes and leaning wearily back.

He wished he'd found some other way.

Chapter 20

Artemis's eyes fluttered open, her black lashes flicking away the residual darkness. She found herself in a confined space, dimly lit and smelling of disinfectant. Her heart thudded against her chest, the pounding echoing inside her skull as she fought to recall how she had arrived here.

"Where...?" she muttered, her voice barely above a whisper.

Her vision swam as she blinked rapidly, trying to clear the fog that gripped her mind.

When she'd thrown herself back at the sound of gunshots, her head had hit the ground. Too hard—consciousness had been fleeting.

The van's metal walls were cold to the touch, and she could feel the vibrations from the engine beneath her fingertips. As her surroundings came into focus, she realized she was lying on a sterile, stainless steel table. Artemis's breath hitched, her memory shuffling through the events that led her here like riffling through a deck of cards.

She steadied her breathing, focusing her analytical mind on piecing together the fragments of her memory. Images flashed before her—a gunshot. The van lurched suddenly, snapping her back to reality and forcing her to confront the implications of her current situation.

As Artemis's vision steadied, she became aware of the familiar face hovering close to her own. Helen's curly brown hair framed her gentle features like a halo, her eyes filled with concern as she studied her younger sister.

"Artemis, are you all right?" Helen asked softly, her voice a soothing balm. She reached out and patted Artemis's cheek gently, the warmth of her touch providing an anchor for Artemis's swimming thoughts.

"I... I think so," Artemis replied, her voice still weak but growing stronger as she regained her bearings. She felt the weight of her sister's worry heavy on her chest, even as she marveled at how Helen managed to maintain her composure despite the whirlwind of events that had just transpired.

"Good, because we don't have much time," Otto interjected, his tone urgent. He pinched Artemis's arm less gently than Helen's touch, his fingers digging into her flesh as though trying to shake her fully awake. "We need to get moving."

Artemis gritted her teeth against the sting of her father's pinch, irritation flaring within her as she pushed herself up from the cold, sterile table. She knew he was right—they couldn't afford to waste any time—but the pain served as a reminder of how precarious their situation was. With each passing second, the danger grew closer, and she could feel the clock ticking down like a time bomb in the back of her mind.

"Alright, I'm up," she snapped, brushing off Otto's hand and swinging her legs over the side of the table. The metal surface beneath her feet was cold, but the chill only served to sharpen her focus. As she surveyed her surroundings, the cramped quarters of the coroner's van seemed to close in around Artemis. She shifted her weight, trying to find a more comfortable position. Her knees brushed against Helen's while Otto loomed above them both, his thin shoulders nearly touching the ceiling. The dim light filtering through the van's narrow windows cast eerie shadows on their faces, adding to the tension that hung heavy in the air.

Artemis noticed an unfamiliar face glancing in the rearview mirror as the driver watched them; he quickly glanced away when he realized he'd been noticed.

"Feels like we're stuffed into a sardine can," Artemis muttered, earning an uneasy chuckle from Helen. The humor did little to alleviate the suffocating atmosphere; it only served to emphasize how out of place they were in this grim setting.

"Needs must," Otto replied cryptically, his gaze flicking between the closed doors at the back of the van and their driver up front, who appeared to be making every effort not to listen to their conversation.

As Artemis shifted again, she felt an odd lump under her blouse. A momentary panic seized her before she remembered the fake blood capsules she'd hidden there. They had gone unnoticed during the inspection for the wire. She'd hidden them in her bra lining.

And now, the capsules had stained her shirt.

The timing had been important. She'd crushed them the moment the gunfire had erupted. They'd rehearsed the timing so many times before Artemis had arrived at the gambling hall.

"Did it work?" she whispered, her voice as delicate as a butterfly's wings. "Did we manage to fake my death?"

Otto gazed at her for a moment, seeming to measure the weight of his answer before finally allowing a sly smirk to play across his lips. The lines around his eyes crinkled in a familiar manner that always made Artemis feel like she was in on some private joke.

"Like a charm," he replied, his tone light but confident. "They took the bait, hook, line, and sinker."

Artemis allowed herself a small sigh of relief, her heart still pounding in her chest. The gambit they had undertaken was nothing short of audacious.

"Are you sure?" she asked, feeling the need for reassurance gnawing at her insides. "We can't afford any mistakes. Not now."

Otto reached across the narrow space, placing a reassuring hand on her shoulder. His touch was firm, grounding her amidst the whirlwind of uncertainty that threatened to consume her.

"Trust me, Artemis," he said, his eyes locking onto hers with unwavering certainty. "I've been in this game long enough to know when we have the upper hand. And right now, we're one step ahead of everyone else."

She nodded, accepting his words as truth. After all, if anyone could pull off such a daring scheme, it was him.

"Good," Artemis said, steeling herself against the challenges that lay ahead.

The sharp swerves and sudden brakes of the coroner's van jolted Artemis back to reality, her eyes darting towards the driver. His gaze remained fixed on the road as he expertly wove through the labyrinth of traffic, the muscles in his jaw tense and his knuckles white from gripping the wheel. Though he feigned ignorance to the conversation that unfolded behind him, his strained posture betrayed his interest.

"Otto," Helen whispered, her voice barely audible even in the close confines of the van. Her wide, fearful eyes were locked onto something at her feet, and Artemis followed her gaze to find a discarded gun resting there like a venomous snake.

"Easy, Helen," Otto said, his voice steady despite the chaos outside their window. "You did what you had to do." He cast a sideways glance at his eldest daughter, assessing her mental state with the practiced eye of someone who'd seen her through countless breakdowns over the years.

Artemis watched as Helen tried to steady her breathing, her chest rising and falling rapidly beneath her rumpled blouse. The gun, she realized, was a physical manifestation of the turmoil that roiled within her sister—a symbol of the violence that they had all been forced to embrace.

Helen had been the one to fire the shots.

255

"Are we safe?" Helen asked, her hands wringing together in her lap. Artemis could see the tremors that shook her slender fingers.

"Safe enough for now," Otto replied, his attention returning to the task at hand. "But we can't let our guard down. Not yet."

Helen nodded, though it was clear that her thoughts were still consumed by the weight of her actions. Artemis felt a surge of protectiveness towards her sister, wishing she could shoulder some of the burden that threatened to crush her.

"Listen," Artemis said, leaning forward so their foreheads nearly touched. "You did what you had to. No one was shot. You took out the windows and gave them a scare. That's it."

Then, her eyes narrowed, "And an FBI agent was killed in Mehmet's office. He's going to pay for Irem's death."

Her father nodded. "I placed the calls when I saw you enter. The police responded surprisingly quickly."

Artemis felt her heart skip a beat as she said, "How's Izel? Any news?"

"Survived. Recovering at the hospital," Helen said, flashing a small, weary smile.

Artemis squeezed her sister's hand, the warmth of their shared bond providing a small measure of comfort amidst the uncertainty that loomed over them. As the van continued its frenzied dance through the city streets, she couldn't help but wonder if she'd made the right choice.

The staccato rhythm of the van's wheels bumping over the uneven streets played a discordant counterpoint to the tension hanging in the air. Helen's breaths came shallow and quick, her gaze locked on the gun that lay beside her feet like an accusation.

"Your aim was spot-on, Helen," Otto said, attempting to break through her distress with a touch of levity. "You'd give any marksman a run for their money."

Helen flinched at his words, a shudder racking her body as she pushed the weapon further away with the toe of her shoe. "I never wanted to be good at this," she mumbled, her voice barely audible above the cacophony of the city outside.

"None of us wanted this," Artemis agreed, her chest tightening with empathy. She watched her sister, struggling to hold back the tears that threatened to spill over her flushed cheeks. "But we're doing what we have to in order to survive."

"Artemis is right," Otto chimed in, his voice gentle yet firm. "We've all had to adapt, learn new skills to stay ahead of those who would see us dead."

"You're still sure this was the right call?" Artemis asked, glancing at her father. "We're leaving that immunity on the table."

Otto snorted. "And to live on that FBI lady's hook all our lives? It's a different type of imprisonment. No. We made the right call. We paid him enough as it is," Otto added, waving a hand towards the driver who was still wearing his paramedic's uniform. He'd been the one to say she was dead. A coroner in the city was lined up to confirm it, and then "cremate" her body. It had all cost them a nice chunk of the money they'd stowed away, but it was worth it.

"Did we hear back..." Artemis said suddenly, glancing at Helen. "From..." she trailed off, her voice full of hope.

But Helen shook her head apologetically. "We still haven't heard from Forester. He should have contacted us by now." Her fingers tapped a restless rhythm against her thigh, betraying a growing unease.

"Perhaps he's simply been delayed," Otto offered, though his frown betrayed his lack of conviction. "We must trust in his resourcefulness."

"Or maybe something's happened to him," Artemis murmured, her gaze darting towards the rearview mirror as if expecting to see Forester's familiar form materialize in the reflection.

"Enough," Otto said decisively. "Speculation will do us no good. We need to focus on our next move and trust that Forester will reach out when he can."

Artemis frowned as deep within her, a seed of doubt took root.

The van swerved around a sharp corner, jolting Artemis out of her thoughts. She straightened up in the narrow space, bracing herself against the van's walls. She wiped away the fake blood that had pooled on her chin, leaving a crimson smudge on the back of her hand.

It was like a slap, jarring her fully to her senses now.

"How many times did you try?"

"What?" her father said.

"Forester. How many times?"

"Forget about him, Artemis."

"No. No, he's part of this."

Otto let out a weary sigh.

Artemis was pulling her own phone from her pocket now, frowning as she did.

No missed messages. No missed calls.

Shit.

Her stomach tightened.

She cycled to Cameron's temporary number he'd been using overseas, and she placed a call.

No response.

She tried again. It went straight to voicemail.

"Forester's not responding," she announced, her voice tight with concern. "We have to find him."

"Artemis," Otto began, his urgency palpable as he spoke, "we can't. We need to leave now, or we risk being caught ourselves. You know our priority is to get to safety. New identities. New passports. It's all waiting at the airfield. That FBI... woman... won't be able to track us."

"I understand, but—" she hesitated, the weight of responsibility heavy on her shoulders. "I can't just abandon him. He could be in danger."

"Listen to me," Otto insisted, his tone firm but laced with a-ffection. "Your sister and I are here for you. We can protect each other, okay?"

Artemis's heart pounded in her chest as she weighed the options before her. The cramped van felt suffocating, and the acrid scent of gunpowder still lingered on her clothing. Helen clutched at her discarded weapon, her eyes wide with anticipation while Otto stared at Artemis expectantly, waiting for her decision.

"Artemis," Helen whispered, her voice trembling, "please, come with us."

"Forester could be injured or worse," Artemis spoke aloud, her gaze fixed on the metal floor of the van. "But if I don't go with you now—" she met her sister's eyes, "—you might never make it to safety."

"Time's running out, Artemis," Otto warned, his gruff voice betraying a hint of desperation.

"Alright," Artemis finally said, reaching a decision that felt like a knife cutting through her conscience. "I need to stay and check on something. Go ahead without me."

"Absolutely not," Otto barked, his eyes blazing. "You're coming with us, and that's final."

"Dad, I can't just—"

"Artemis!" he snapped, silencing her protest. "This is not up for debate. You're my daughter, and I won't let you put yourself in even more danger."

"Dad," Helen interjected, her voice surprisingly steady, "she's made her choice. We have to trust her."

"Trust her?" Otto spat, his face inches from hers. "This isn't a game! This is life and death!"

"Exactly," Helen replied, her chin lifting defiantly. "And we all have to make our own choices. She's given up everything. She was the only one with a normal life. And I've ruined it. For everyone." Helen stared off into the distance.

"No!" Artemis said firmly. "You're worth it, Helen. We're going to start over. I promise. But I can't abandon Cameron."

A heavy silence fell over the van as the words sank in. Artemis caught her father's gaze, pleading silently for understanding. Finally, Otto sighed, the fight draining from him.

"Fine," he conceded, his voice thick with emotion. "But if anything happens—"

"Nothing will," Artemis interrupted, her determination resolute. "I'll find Forester and meet you at the rendezvous point. I promise."

"Alright," Otto said, giving her a somber nod.

Helen spoke something in Turkish to the driver, and he pulled over to the side of the road.

With her decision made, Artemis swung open the van's rear door and leapt out, landing firmly on the asphalt. The cold air rushed past her cheeks, her breath visible in the crisp night air.

"Artemis, reconsider... what if—" Otto shouted after her, his voice wrought with concern. But she didn't look back nor hear the rest of what he'd said as she shut the door. Her focus was singular, driven by a fierce determination to find Forester and ensure his safety.

As she broke into a run back towards the city, her mind raced with thoughts and questions, each one more urgent than the last. Where was Forester? Was he hurt, or worse? Had their plan to fake her death even worked as intended?

"Focus," she whispered to herself, her breaths coming in short, sharp pants. "One step at a time."

Slowing her pace, Artemis fished her phone from her pocket and dialed for a taxi. She knew that relying on public transportation would only slow her down further. Time was of the essence, and she couldn't afford any delays.

It was only now, as she stood there, as her senses returned, and as the fog in her mind cleared that she realized...

Grant had said someone was coming after Cameron.

What if that someone had found Forester?

Artemis felt another, horrible shiver jolt down her spine.

CHAPTER 21

ARTEMIS SAT RIGIDLY IN the back of the taxi cab, her coal-black hair a stark contrast to the ivory skin on her flushed cheeks. The clamor of Istanbul's streets did nothing to alleviate the crushing weight of her fears.

Her phone was clutched in her hand like a lifeline. Forester still wasn't answering.

It had taken so damn long to get the taxi, and now they were driving back in the direction of the gated site.

Her heart raced as she clutched onto her phone, her fingers trembling with urgency. With each second that ticked by, Forester's life hung in a precarious balance. She could still see him in her mind's eye—the tall, scarred man with disheveled hair and the ever-present mischievous glint.

Her heart panged at the thought of never seeing him again.

"Alright, enough," she muttered under her breath, reprimanding herself for the direction of her thoughts. Artemis unlocked her phone and hastily typed a message for the tenth time in the last hour, the words flowing from her fingertips as if they held the power to save a life.

Forester... Please. Reply. I don't want to break up. Please!

She stared at the screen. A small portion of her mind knew that the phone Forester was using was a burner. It meant that no one would be able to trace it and realize the stunt with the coroner's van and fake shootout was all a mirage.

But though her family depended on the ruse to work—or at least to keep Agent Grant confused enough that she stopped meddling—Artemis found she wasn't so concerned over it anymore.

She just needed to find Cameron.

The last ten text messages had gone unanswered. She re-read them, noticing how they grew more and more urgent with each subsequent message:

"Forester, where are you?"

"Please, let me know you're okay."

"I'm getting worried, Forester. Please respond."

"Forester, this isn't funny. Please answer me."

"Forester, I didn't mean anything I said. Please. Just call back..."

"Forester, I'm serious. This isn't a joke anymore."

She stared at the phone, heart in her throat. He wasn't answering. He hadn't been answering.

But her name wasn't stored in his new burner phone. He'd only just gotten it the previous day when they'd landed.

She frowned. Which meant what, exactly?

... Agent Grant had gone on about some assassin, someone who'd targeted Forester.

And her.

Artemis had also been in the crossfire. The only card she had, then was herself. She wet her bottom lip slowly, nervously, staring at her phone. And then, with trembling fingers, she tried something else...

"This is Artemis Blythe. If you want me, you'll have to tell me where you are."

"Please, let this work," she silently pleaded. As a keen observer of human nature, she knew all too well that the person who had taken Forester would be driven by a potent blend of arrogance and ambition. It was this knowledge that gave her hope—hope that her message would reach its intended recipient and that it would be enough to buy Forester time.

But time was the one thing she knew they had very little of.

With a deep breath, Artemis pressed the send button, releasing her desperate message into the void. She clutched the phone to her chest, praying silently that it would reach its destination and provide the leverage needed to save Forester.

"Please," she whispered, her voice barely audible above the hum of the taxi's engine.

Outside, Istanbul flowed past her window like a living tapestry. The city was a vibrant, chaotic dance of people and vehicles, all vying for space amidst the maze of narrow streets and ancient buildings. But despite the captivating panorama, Artemis's thoughts remained firmly anchored to the man who had been snatched from her life—and whom she now sought to reclaim.

As the taxi weaved through the press of nighttime cars, buses, and pedestrians, Artemis's heart pounded in sync with the rhythm of the city. She knew that every second that passed brought Forester closer to an uncertain fate, and the knowledge fueled her determination.

"Driver, can you go any faster?" she asked, her voice taut with urgency. She still couldn't quite see the building where they'd been staying. Was there a chance Cameron was there? Maybe his phone had died and he was waiting for her.

"Come on," she muttered, her eyes fixed on the device as though willing it to spring to life. "Give me something to work with."

Yet, despite her fierce concentration, the silence stretched on, each tick of the clock mocking her efforts and deepening her apprehension. And as the taxi continued its slow crawl through Istanbul's teeming streets, Artemis Blythe found herself locked in a battle not just against time, but against her own fears and doubts.

In the dim light of the taxi's interior, Artemis watched the cityscape morph into a blur of vibrant colors and unfamiliar shapes. The cacophony of honking horns and shouting vendors only added to the disorienting effect, leaving her feeling isolated within the vehicle's confines. As minutes stretched into an eternity, she fidgeted with her phone, her thumb hovering over the screen in anxious expectation.

"Please," she whispered, as though her plea could somehow reach Forester through the ether and hasten his response.

Artemis knew that time was slipping away, each second another grain of sand in an hourglass rapidly emptying.

"Miss? Are you okay?" the driver asked in broken English, glancing at her through the rearview mirror.

"Fine," she answered curtly, unwilling to be drawn into conversation. Her focus remained fixed on her phone, willing it to provide some vital piece of information.

As if in answer to her unspoken prayer, the device suddenly lit up, its shrill ringtone shattering the silence. Her heart leaped into her throat, and she fumbled to answer the call, her fingers trembling with a mixture of desperation and determination.

"Hello?" she said, her voice wavering slightly despite her best efforts to remain composed.

"Artemis Blythe," came the reply, cold and detached.

"Who is this? What do you want?" she demanded, her eyes narrowing as she struggled to keep her emotions in check. This most definitely was not Cameron's voice.

"Ah, so assertive," the voice taunted, a cruel smile evident in its tone. "How refreshing."

"Enough games," she snapped, her patience wearing thin. "Where is Forester?"

"Patience, my dear. All in good time." The man's arrogance oozed through the phone, fueling her anger and terror.

This confirmed it.

What she'd feared most.

Forester was in trouble... was he... was he...

She couldn't even complete the thought.

She swallowed, feeling her stomach twist in on itself.

"Tell me now, or I swear I'll—"

"Watch your tone, Miss Blythe," he interrupted, his words laced with menace. "You're hardly in a position to make demands."

Artemis clenched her jaw, swallowing her pride. She knew that, for now, she had no choice but to play by this man's rules.

"Fine," she conceded, forcing herself to adopt a more conciliatory tone. "What do you want from me? Who are you? Are you the one that went into my apartment?"

"Oh... you have been doing your homework. Clever trick, taking a private flight the day earlier." A chortle, then a loud, pronounced swallow. She could practically see a sweaty Adam's apple rising and falling.

"What do you want?" she repeated, more firmly this time.

"Simple: a meeting," he replied. "Be at the first Bosphorus Bridge in one hour." And with that, the line went dead.

The reflection of neon lights on the rain-soaked streets filled the taxi with an eerie glow, casting distorted shadows across Artemis's face. Her heart raced as she pressed the phone to her ear, her voice wavering between desperation and determination.

"Hello?"

No reply.

"Hello!" she said, louder and more urgently.

But he'd hung up.

Terror welled in her chest.

The cacophony of Istanbul's streets fell away as Artemis stared at her phone, the screen now dark after the chilling ultimatum. She took a deep breath, attempting to quell the storm of emotions that threatened to overwhelm her. In that moment, she knew she had to face this dangerous game alone; involving anyone else could jeopardize Forester's life and her own.

"First Bosphorus Bridge!" she exclaimed, adrenaline coursing through her veins as she snapped back to reality. "Take me there, now!"

"Of course," the taxi driver replied, his dark eyes meeting hers in the rearview mirror for a brief moment before he swerved into the chaotic traffic, leaving a deluge of honking horns in their wake.

As the taxi sped through the city, weaving between buses and pedestrians with reckless abandon, Artemis's thoughts raced alongside it, trying to formulate a plan. She couldn't shake the image of Forester, bound and at the mercy of this cruel adversary. Every tick of the clock seemed to mock her, reminding her of the precious time slipping away.

"Can't you go any faster?" she demanded, clutching the door handle as if her life depended on it.

"Doing my best, miss," the driver responded, dodging another vehicle with surprising dexterity.

Artemis bit her lip, willing herself to think clearly despite the rising panic. She needed a strategy that would outmaneuver her opponent and ensure Forester's safety. But with so little information, even her strategic mind struggled to find a solution. She closed her eyes, focusing on the sound of her own heartbeat.

"Here we are," the driver announced suddenly, jolting Artemis out of her thoughts. The first Bosphorus Bridge loomed ahead, its steel cables etched against the twilight sky like a giant spider's web.

"Wait for me," she ordered, her voice firm as she handed him a generous payment. "I'll be back soon." She didn't know if that was a promise or a prayer.

"Of course," he replied, nodding solemnly. "Good luck."

Artemis stepped out of the taxi, the cold wind whipping her coal-black hair against her pale cheeks. She gazed at the bridge, an electric anxiety making her fidget in place. This was it. No fallback. No clever outs.

Whether she or Forester lived another day would be decided here.

CHAPTER 22

THE WIND WHIPPED AT Artemis as she stepped onto the bridge, her eyes scanning the desolate walkways. Though devoid of people, cars continued to barrel across the bridge, their headlights casting eerie shadows on the concrete surface and adding to the sense of urgency and danger that gripped her.

"Damn it, Forester," she muttered under her breath. "Where are you?" Each passing second gnawed at her resolve like a ravenous animal. She felt exposed, vulnerable—a pawn on the edge of the board, far from her usual command as a chess master.

As if responding to her thoughts, a car sped past her with a sudden roar, startling Artemis. She instinctively flattened herself against the bridge's railing, her breaths coming in ragged gasps. Her mind raced, attempting to stay several moves ahead despite the unnerving circumstances. Could the kidnapper be watching me right now?

"Think, Artemis, think," she whispered to herself, her fingers tracing the cool metal of the railing. The sound of tires screeching in the distance jolted her into action. It could be nothing, a simple coincidence. But it could also be the sign she so desperately needed.

"Forester!" she shouted, her voice carried away by the wind. No response came, but she refused to give in to despair.

"Come on, you bastard," she growled, addressing the unseen kidnapper. "Give me something to work with." Though she tried to appear unfazed, her desperation grew with each passing moment. Time was slipping through her fingers like sand, and she knew that every tick of the clock brought Forester closer to danger.

She broke into a run along the side of the bridge. The rhythmic pounding of her footsteps on the pavement drowned out the sound of cars rushing past, their headlights casting fleeting shadows that danced across her face. Her chest tightened with each labored breath, but she forced herself to keep moving, scanning the dark expanse in both directions for any sign of Forester or the kidnapper.

"Come on," she muttered under her breath, her voice barely audible over the roar of the river below. "Where are you?"

As she continued running, Artemis' thoughts raced alongside her, analyzing every possible scenario, every potential clue. She couldn't afford to miss anything; the stakes were too high. And in this twisted game of cat and mouse, she couldn't help but feel like she was always one step behind.

"Forester! Can you hear me?" she yelled, her voice echoing through the chilly night air.

No response. Just the relentless hum of traffic and the distant murmur of the city beyond.

Clenching her fists, Artemis willed herself to focus. This was no time for panic. She had faced down danger before, and she would do it again. But as the seconds ticked away, her fear threatened to overpower her logic.

"Damn it," she whispered, gritting her teeth. "I need something. Anything."

And then, almost as if in answer to her silent plea, she saw it: an oddly shaped shadow dangling over the edge of the bridge.

She stared at it.

The shadow swayed.

A large shadow.

Far too large...

Her heart went still.

At first glance, it seemed to be a body hanging limply, swaying gently in the breeze. Artemis's heart caught in her throat at the sight, her stomach twisting into knots.

"Forester?" she called hesitantly, approaching the figure with trepidation.

A car behind her blared its horn, and she jolted. But the vehicle sped on by.

Artemis's breath hitched as her eyes locked onto the strange object. She steeled herself, knowing she had to investigate. One foot in front of the other, she moved closer, along the edge of the bridge, hand trailing on the cold iron rail as if she needed it to brace herself or risk falling; her mind racing through all possible scenarios. The air was thick with tension, and the sound of her own heartbeat seemed deafening.

"Forester?" she whispered, hoping against hope that it wasn't him. Her legs trembled slightly, but she forced them to stay steady. This was no time for weakness.

As she neared the edge, Artemis squinted her eyes, trying to discern the details.

The object swayed back and forth, the rhythm almost hypnotic. And then, suddenly, clarity struck like a bolt of lightning.

Or, rather, a flash of lightning—coming from a truck barreling down the bridge.

A sweeping beam illuminated the thing dangling there.

At first, she felt a flood of relief.

Then fear.

It wasn't a body; it was a sack tied to a noose.

A lumpy, old, burlap sack.

She could almost hear the creek of the rope swaying.

She stared at it, frowning.

A decoy.

But a decoy from what?

"Damn it!" she hissed, slamming her fist against the bridge railing.

Frustration and confusion washed over Artemis like an icy wave, chilling her to the core. She glanced around, taking in the empty walkways and the distant hum of traffic, searching for something—anything—that could provide a clue. Her mind worked at a frenetic pace, calculating angles and probabilities, trying to make sense of this nightmarish situation.

She whispered, her voice barely audible above the wind that whipped through her hair. "Where are you?"

Her eyes darted back and forth as she paced along the bridge's edge, frustration mounting with each moment that passed. Time was running out, and she knew it.

CHAPTER 23

A SHARP PAIN PIERCED through Cameron Forester's skull, dragging him back into consciousness. He gasped for air as the throbbing ache intensified, his vision swimming in and out of focus. With each thud of his heartbeat, the pain crescendoed, threatening to split his head open.

"Awake at last, I see," a voice drawled from the shadows.

Forester tried to move, but the coarse, ragged bindings digging into his wrists and ankles made it clear he was bound tightly to a chair. Panic set in as he struggled to recall what had led him to this dimly lit room. His mouth felt like parchment, and the coppery taste of blood lingered on his tongue.

"Wh-where am I?" he croaked, gritting his teeth against the relentless pounding in his head.

"Does it really matter?" The voice sneered but offered no further explanation.

Forester strained to see through the murky darkness, his eyes struggling to adjust to the scant light that seeped through the grimy windows. As his vision cleared, he took stock of his battered body. His once pristine shirt was now torn and bloodied, clinging to his bruised torso like a second skin. His disheveled hair hung in damp clumps around his face, evidence of the cold sweat that covered him.

"Who... who are you?" he demanded, scorn instead of fear lacing his words.

It wasn't that he didn't feel afraid, but somewhere between his mind and his tongue, the words transformed into defiance.

Much of his life had been marked with this particular trait.

"Patience, Mr. Forester," the voice replied coolly. "All will be revealed soon enough."

Forester fought to keep the fear at bay, his mind racing with questions. How did they know his name, and what did they want with him?

"Why don't you unchain me, huh? I'll give you a run for your money. How about it?"

The voice laughed, a cruel and chilling sound that sent shivers down Forester's spine. "I doubt that, Mr. Forester," it sneered. "But I must admit, it is quite entertaining to see you squirm."

The dim light in the room seemed to flicker, casting eerie shadows on the walls. Forester's pulse raced as he strained to see through the darkness. It was then that he noticed a figure standing by the window, silhouetted against the faint moonlight. The man held a rifle, its barrel gleaming with an unsettling menace.

"About time you joined me," the figure said, his voice cold and detached. "I was beginning to think I'd have to wake you up myself."

As the man stepped forward into the light, Forester's eyes widened in disbelief.

A ghost stared back at him.

A very ugly ghost.

An ugly, stupid, evil, pathetic, waste of space, piece-of-shit ghost.

"Shit," was all Forester managed to say.

He blinked, certain he was dreaming. But this motion caused his face to ache. He'd been beaten, apparently. He could feel the bruises on his skin—like after a cage fight.

His head also throbbed. Likely from part beating and part alcohol. A concoction he wasn't entirely unfamiliar with.

Before him stood Ethan Warwick, a man he had believed dead – killed by his own hand in their last encounter. Forester's heart hammered in his chest, his thoughts racing in a futile attempt to make sense of what he was seeing.

"Ethan?" he stammered, his mind grappling with the ghost from his past. Then, deciding the name was too humanizing, he added, "You stupid son of a bitch. What are you doing on this side of the dirt, you bastard?"

"Clearly not dead enough for your liking," Ethan replied, a twisted grin stretching across his face.

Forester felt a wave of rage surge through him, but he fought to keep his emotions in check. He couldn't let Ethan know how deeply his presence unsettled him. "What do you want, Warwick?" he asked, his voice barely concealing the tremble within. "Warwick," he repeated. "You know, no matter how many times I repeat it, that name doesn't get any less stupid."

"You never were as funny as you thought."

"As far as expectations go, you're as ugly as I remember."

Ethan sneered, pacing slowly around the room, his rifle never straying far from Forester's body. "I'm going to enjoy what I do to you. It's going to take us some time, mind you. Maybe weeks. Months." He purred, almost like a cat in a beam of sunlight.

Forester's mind raced, trying to piece together the jigsaw puzzle of events that had transpired since his capture. He couldn't afford to let Ethan see any hint of vulnerability. His thoughts flitted like a moth to a flame, searching for any opening, any opportunity to turn the tables on his captor.

"Damn. What happened to your hand?" Forester said, chipper and cheerful.

"Oh... the same thing that happened to your beloved, I'd guess. Have you ever imagined what she sounded like as I killed her? I'm sure you've imagined her screaming or crying... she moaned. Do you know how she sounded when she moaned? Perhaps you'd like to hear where I cut her first, hmm? There was nothing dignified about it. No theatrical cries of pain. She squealed, Cameron. Like a sow. You're more used to pain than she was. But I'm going to make you squeal like her... though... I'm not sure you'll be as shrill." He tapped a prosthetic finger against his lips. "I bet you I still have the video of what I did to her. We had a lot of fun. Well... at least... I did."

He winked.

Cameron tried to break through the cuffs and the chair; one moment, sitting idle, the next, howling and surging forward with a snarl.

But his wrists ached against the chains binding him. He felt his bones protest as if threatening to go out of socket or break. This didn't stop him, though, he continued to roar and kick and try to force himself from his bindings by sheer force of will.

But skin against metal wasn't a very fair fight.

He collapsed again, his wrists both bleeding, his chest heaving and sweat pouring down his face.

Ethan Warwick just watched him, allowing his amusement to crease his features.

Forester wasn't sure what bum luck was, but he knew he had it.

The man he had thought dead now stood before him, smug and lethal.

"Comfortable?" Ethan asked, a wicked grin playing on his lips as he leaned against the windowsill, cradling the rifle in his arms.

"Never been better," Forester retorted, trying to keep his voice steady. His mind raced with strategies and possibilities even as he clenched his jaw against the pulsating pain in his head. "You know, tying me up seems like overkill. Afraid I might hurt your feelings?"

"Always the joker, aren't you?" Ethan chuckled, but there was a dangerous edge to his laughter. "But no, it's not about that. I just want you to have a front-row seat to the show."

Gritting his teeth, Forester summoned every ounce of strength he possessed and tugged at the chains binding his wrists. The coarse metal bit into his flesh, but the pain only fueled his determination. If he could free himself, he could still gain the upper hand—or at least, that's what he told himself as sweat broke out across his brow and his muscles trembled with exertion.

"Give it up, Forester," Ethan taunted, clearly enjoying the spectacle. "Those cuffs are tighter than a miser's purse strings."

Forester muttered under his breath, twisting his wrists in an effort to work the cuffs loose. His fingers grew numb from the strain, but he refused to surrender.

In his mind's eye, Forester envisioned the precise movements he needed to make, the subtle shifts and turns that might grant him a sliver of hope.

But nothing.

His bones groaned in protest as he stretched his arms to their max.

Ethan's laughter reverberated through the room, a cruel symphony to Forester's pain. "Look at you," he taunted, circling the bound man like a vulture tracking its prey. "I never thought I'd see the great Cameron Forester reduced to this—a helpless, pathetic mess."

Forester gritted his teeth, his jaw muscles clenching with the effort of maintaining his stoic facade. He refused to give Ethan the satisfaction of seeing him break.

"Tell me, Forester," Ethan continued, his voice a venomous whisper as he leaned in close, "how does it feel? To be completely at my mercy?"

"Enjoy it while it lasts," Forester replied through gritted teeth.

"Ah, always the optimist," Ethan mused, his hand slipping into his pocket and emerging with a gleaming knife. The blade caught the dim light, casting eerie shadows on the walls. "But let's not forget who holds the power here."

With a swift, practiced movement, Ethan flicked the knife toward Forester's face. The cold steel sliced through skin, drawing a thin line of blood down his cheek. Forester winced but refused to cry out, his eyes locked onto Ethan's in silent defiance.

"Such bravery," Ethan mocked, wiping the bloodied blade on his pant leg. "Or just plain stupidity?"

"Go to hell."

"Haven't you noticed?" Another flick of the knife, and another flash of pain. "We're already here."

The ex-soldier smirked as he wiped the bloody knife off on Forester's chest.

Sweat trickled down Cameron's brow, stinging his freshly cut cheek and pooling at the base of his throat. He gritted his teeth, muscles tensing and releasing in a futile effort to loosen the bindings that held him captive.

"Speaking of entertainment," Ethan continued, shifting his weight onto one leg, "I saw Artemis earlier." He paused, letting the name hang in the air between them like a noose. "She's on the bridge right now, probably wondering where in the world her knight in shining armor has gone."

He raised his rifle, peering through the scope. "Ah, there she is. Shuffling around like a little hen. Cluck little hen. Cluck." He turned to Cameron, beaming. "Would you like to see?"

Forester just stared, horror welling inside him.

The scope of the rifle was pressed, none too gently, against his face.

He didn't want to look, but he couldn't help himself.

Through the lens, he saw her. She was standing on the bridge, her eyes wide with fear and confusion. She looked so small, so vulnerable.

At first, he'd half hoped Warwick had been mistaken. That he'd lured the wrong woman.

But no... Artemis was too smart. She would've found him. If anyone could've, it was her.

In that moment, Forester knew he would do whatever it took to protect her. He had to get out of this mess.

Forester's heart skipped a beat, panic lacing his veins with ice.

"Ah, now there's a reaction," Ethan observed, his eyes gleaming with malicious delight. "I must say, I've been looking forward to our little reunion. It's been far too long since we last crossed paths."

"Stay away from her," Forester growled, the words escaping him like a feral snarl.

"Or what? You'll stop me?"

"I will kill you."

"Hmm. You tried that already. Remember?"

As the cold reality of his situation settled over him, Forester knew that he was running out of time. If he couldn't find a way to escape the cuffs and this godforsaken room, Artemis would be lost to him forever.

"Tick-tock, Forester," Ethan taunted, his voice dripping with sadistic glee. "You know what they say about a watched pot never boiling."

"Here... why don't I just wing her first? Which leg, I'll let you choose. Come now, or I'll go center mass. Tell me which leg, Cameron."

He raised his rifle, scope pressed to his cheek. A self-satisfied smirk crossed his features.

Forester knew the bastard was a good shot. A very good one.

"Damn you!" Forester spat, muscles bulging beneath the taut chains that held him captive. He gritted his teeth, the pain in his head flaring like white-hot fire as he pulled against the unyielding cuffs.

"Such language," Ethan chided. "Give me a leg, Cameron, or I'll decapitate your new squeeze."

Ethan's malicious laughter hung in the air like a ghastly specter, and every second that ticked by weighed on Forester like an anchor dragging him deeper into the abyss. His breathing came in ragged gasps, sweat pouring down his face as he strained against the chains binding him to the chair. Artemis's life was at stake, and he couldn't—wouldn't—let her down.

He spotted as the soldier began to squeeze the trigger.

One bullet. One small piece of lead was all that separated Forester from a life of eternal misery.

A very short one, albeit.

All that remained between Artemis Blythe and death was his force of will.

He had no choice.

The cuffs would rip his wrist, break his bones, shatter his fingers. His hand would never be the same again.

But he was strong.

And right now, his damn hand was an obstacle. He howled with rage, adrenaline coursing through him, and he lunged forward, ripping his hand through the cuff.

He felt his thumb break. His wrist shattered. Two of his fingers as well.

It was hard to keep track of all the damage.

Pain flared like fire from his fingertips to his shoulder. As Forester tore his arm free, the chair he'd been bound to toppled over with a loud crash. Ethan's attention snapped toward the noise, and for a split second, his guard was down, and his gun went just a hair higher.

A shot.

A loud retort of the blast through the room.

But he had missed—he had to have missed, Cameron thought, the fleeting notion feeling like pleading with fate.

It would have to be enough.

His pain, his hand, was all he had to offer.

Now, one of his wrists was still cuffed, and the other was a useless, mangled thing, torn fingers shivering with the shock and nerve damage.

"Damn you, Forester!" Ethan snarled, confirming, to Cameron's utmost relief, that he had missed his shot. He glared at Forester, who sat smirking on the floor despite his broken hand and the throbbing pain that pulsed through his body.

The blood was flowing freely from his wrist now. His mind was fading, his thoughts spinning.

"Seems I'm full of surprises," Forester quipped, gritting his teeth against the agony.

All he had left was defiance.

Too much pain. Nothing left in the tank—just agony.

Ethan's nostrils flared, and his grip tightened on the rifle. He aimed again, sighting through his scope, then cursed again. Forester could no longer see, but he hoped this meant Artemis had taken cover.

"Think you're clever, don't you?" Ethan spat, a dangerous edge to his voice.

Forester didn't respond, focusing instead on the throbbing pain in his head and the fire that seared through his shattered limb.

Ethan snarled, swinging the butt of his rifle violently into Forester's battered face.

The impact sent a shockwave of agony through Forester's skull, but he refused to cry out. Screaming would only serve to enrage Ethan further, and he couldn't risk that. Instead, he let the pain wash over him, using it as a reminder of what was at stake.

Forester's vision blurred, but he focused on the memory of Artemis's face, allowing it to ground him in the present.

It lasted a second.

Then the rifle struck him again.

He tried to raise his hand, but... shit, oh yeah. the thing was already a mess.

Pain lanced up his mushy arm where the rifle struck the upraised appendage. Cameron's vision swam in pulsing, light-headed waves as shocks of pain drove the breath from his body, the black fringe of unconsciousness tugging at the edges of his vision.

Another blow.

Another.

Another.

CHAPTER 24

ARTEMIS STOOD ON THE bridge, staring at the ominous sight before her. A large bag dangled from a noose, swinging like a pendulum over the dark waters of the Bosphorus below. The sinister scene sent an icy shiver down her spine. With every sway of the bag, the urgency to act grew more pressing in her mind.

As she carefully surveyed the surroundings, searching desperately for something... anything, there was a sudden and unmistakable sound.

The sharp crack of a gunshot pierced through the noise of the city. Artemis felt the bullet whiz past her ear, narrowly missing her; it struck the railing, sending sparks through the air.

A miss. A narrow miss, but a miss.

In a split second, her instincts kicked in, and she dove behind a nearby pillar, her heart in a constant pounding rhythm.

"Damn it!" she hissed, her thoughts racing as adrenaline coursed through her veins.

She pressed her back against the concrete pillar.

None of the cars on the bridge seemed to have realized what had happened.

They continued to surge past, leaning on their horns or speeding around each other.

She'd often heard traffic lights in Istanbul were more recommendation than law, but now she believed the rumors.

Artemis crouched low and scanned the area, searching for any sign of the shooter. Her keen eyes caught the faintest glint of metal from a distant window—the top floor of a building facing the bridge.

Still no more gunshots.

Had she been mistaken?

She stared at the building where she'd spotted the glint. It was gone now...

What if she was mistaken?

What if Forester was—

"NO!" she said out loud.

The distance between her and the building was considerable, and there was no telling what awaited her inside. But if the kidnapper was indeed there, she couldn't afford to waste any time. She had to act, and she had to do it now.

If she arose from cover, she'd get shot.

No going right—it would just take her to the other end of the bridge, further away from the shooter. No going left, either.

Only one choice then.

"Here goes nothing," muttered Artemis, steeling herself for what was to come.

The moonlight danced across the water as Artemis took a deep breath and leaped from the bridge.

A brief instance where a gunshot might have resounded—but there was none.

Time seemed to slow down as she plummeted towards the churning waves below.

As she sliced through the water like a dagger. Something brushed against her leg, and Artemis gasped. She thrashed her limbs, her heart racing as she tried to get to the surface. She broke through the water finally, gasping for air as she looked up at the bridge she had just jumped off of.

The water was cold—very cold. It slicked her face, plastering her hair against her features with sheer wetness.

There was no time to waste. Forester was in danger, and she had to hurry. She scythed towards the shore, her muscles straining with the effort.

Her fingers dug into the muddy bank as she pulled herself out of the water. Shivering, soaked to the bone, and aware of the danger lurking above, Artemis knew that her next move could very well determine their fates.

She scrambled to her feet, her clothes clinging to her body, her hair dripping wet. She looked up at the building where she had seen the glint of metal, her eyes narrowed.

With a grimace, Artemis launched herself up the muddy incline, her sneakers slipping and sliding underfoot. The stench of dead jellyfish filled her nostrils as she leaped over a putrid pile of their remains, their once-glistening bodies now reduced to a sickly, rotting mass.

Reaching the base of the building, she found herself confronted with a set of narrow stairs that seemed to stretch on forever.

Drawing on reserves of energy she didn't know she had, Artemis hurled herself up the steps, taking them four at a time as her heart pounded in her ears.

Gasping for breath, Artemis reached the top floor and instantly heard the sounds of commotion coming from the door centering the hall.

It was closed, sealed shut.

In that instant, her eyes locked onto a fire extinguisher mounted on the wall. She seized it, gripping its cold metal surface tightly, and without hesitation, she charged toward the door from which the sounds of violence emanated.

"Forester!" Artemis cried out, her voice laced with both fear and panic. With a final surge of adrenaline, she swung the extinguisher like a battering ram, shattering the door handle which ripped from a bed of splinters as she burst into the dimly lit room.

It took her mind only a second to process the scene.

Forester on the ground. Motionless.

A man above him, rifle in hand.

The man's gaze flickered to her.

His eyes widened. He raised his rifle.

She swiftly aimed the extinguisher at him, releasing a torrent of blinding white foam.

"Argh!" he howled, clawing at his eyes, but Artemis showed no mercy. She swung the extinguisher with all her strength, the impact reverberating through her arms as it connected with the side of his head.

He stumbled back but remained standing.

Forester wasn't moving, lying with a bent arm in a bloody pool.

She glimpsed a flicker of motion from the reeling aggressor.

Artemis' instincts kicked in as she dove to the side, narrowly evading the bullet that zipped past her, grazing her shoulder. She winced at the sharp pain but couldn't afford to dwell on it; there would be time for that later. The acrid smell of gunpowder filled the room, mingling with the bitter taste of adrenaline flooding her mouth.

No time to give him another shot.

No time to think.

She charged forward, closing the distance between them with surprising speed.

As their bodies collided, the gun clattered to the floor, but Artemis quickly found herself grappling with an opponent who was far more skilled than she had anticipated. She could feel each muscle in her body straining as she tried to wrestle him into submission, her breath coming in ragged gasps.

The attacker hissed, suddenly shifting his weight and using Artemis's own momentum against her. The floor rushed up to meet her as she fell hard onto her back, gasping for air and cursing herself for underestimating him.

In a fast motion, the man retrieved his weapon.

The glint of the gun barrel, inches from Artemis's temple, momentarily blinded her as panic clawed at her insides. Her breaths came short and shallow like a wounded animal.

"Forester," the attacker sneered, gasping, his voice dripping with venom, "I have something I'd like you to see."

A blur of movement caught her eye. Forester, who moments ago seemed unconscious, sprang into action with the ferocity of a caged lion finally released. He lunged at the attacker, driving his elbow into the man's face and sending him reeling backward, his grip on the gun faltering.

Behind him, Cameron dragged a metal chair, still cuffed to one hand—his other hand was bent at an impossible angle.

The force of Forester's momentum sent the attacker stumbling towards the shattered window, his footing becoming precarious. Artemis watched in wide-eyed horror as Forester delivered one final blow to the killer's chest, a desperate push that was equal parts fury and hope.

"Go to hell!" Forester roared, his voice ragged from exertion.

The attacker's eyes widened with terror as he crashed through the fragmented glass, but as he fell, he caught Forester's collar, yanking him.

The same ferocious momentum that had aided him now turned on him.

Cameron cried out, tried to brace himself against the window with his mangled hand, but then yelped in pain as it gave out under him like putty.

The sound of shattering glass mingled with the screams that tore through the night air as both men toppled in a tangle over the railing.

"Forester!" Artemis cried out, her legs propelling her to the edge of the balcony. She peered down, her heart caught in her throat, bracing herself for the sight of her friend's mangled form.

Forester grunted, dangling under her. The chair, which was still cuffed to his good hand, had lodged between the bars, holding him up like an anchor. "Thank God," she whispered, relief washing over her like a tidal wave. She reached down, extending her hand to him. "Hold on, I've got you."

"Make it quick," Forester managed through gritted teeth, his grip wavering.

Bracing her feet and leveraging the chair, Artemis brought Forester's good arm in reach of the balcony rail until he snatched hold. Together, they slowly hauled him up and over the railing, collapsing side by side onto the floor in a tangle of limbs and shattered glass.

Artemis' heart pounded furiously as she blinked back hot tears, her chest heaving with relief. The metallic taste of fear still lingered on her tongue. Forester's face, contorted with pain and slick with sweat, was a sight that simultaneously filled her with anguish and gratitude.

"Easy," she whispered gently, trying to soothe him as she pulled the chair upright and began to move the metal ring on his wrist further down so it wasn't biting into his forearm.

"Damn cuffs," Forester growled, fighting back a grimace as circulation returned to his fingers. "They're a real pain in the ass... or, you know. Wrist." He let out a faint gasp of pain.

"Focus on breathing," Artemis ordered, her voice wavering slightly. "And for God's sake, don't crack jokes right now." Her hands shook as they worked, but she didn't let her fear show, adopting the poker face she had mastered through years of high-stakes chess matches.

He was leaning back, his eyes closed. "He dead?"

"What?"

"He dead?" Forester repeated.

"I don't know."

"CHECK!"

The sudden explosion of emotion caught her off guard.

She released her grasp on his wrist, though, and looked over the railing.

A broken body lay on the ground far, far below.

The neck twisted at an impossible angle. His arm, strangely, was ten feet from his body.

No... not his arm. It glinted under the moonlight. A prosthetic limb.

Artemis stared over the edge, swallowing.

305

"Who—who was that?"

"A ghost."

"Really, Cameron. Who was it?"

"No one. He's dead. Right?"

"Yeah. Yeah, he's dead."

Cameron let out a weak, moaning sigh. And then his eyes fluttered as he slipped from consciousness.

EPILOGUE

ARTEMIS WATCHED AS FORESTER massaged his wrist. He stared down at the cast, then looked up again towards the paramedic sitting in the front seat of the van.

"What the hell is this?" Cameron snapped.

"Pain meds seem to be working," Otto muttered.

Artemis just leaned back in the passenger seat, exhausted, and watching her boyfriend slowly come alive as the mountain of pain medication he'd taken took its effect.

The paramedic had done well enough, she thought. She supposed with the amount of money they'd paid him to help fake her death, they were owed a bit of a bonus.

"Why pink?" Cameron snapped. "Hmm? Why the hell is my cast pink?"

"Can I sign it?" Helen called from where she sat in the middle seat.

"Har har," Forester said, but then he winced, wheezing at the ceiling.

"Let it go, tough guy," Otto said, slapping Forester on the shoulder and eliciting another gasp of pain. "You had thirty-two broken bones. In just your forearm and hand."

"Is that a new world record?" Cameron wheezed.

"For stupid prizes, yes," Otto retorted.

Cameron smirked, flashing a thumbs-up with his good hand.

He was a sight to see, leaning back in the back seat, hopped up on pain meds, but still very much alive.

His face was a mangle of bruises and cuts. His arms were scraped with glass and chain marks. And his left arm was a complete mess.

The paramedic had seemed to think the arm would never make a full recovery, but Artemis didn't mention this part to Cameron.

Instead, she leaned back, allowing a slow burst of relief to flood her.

She'd been on the move so much, she hadn't realized how exhausted she was.

Now, she turned, peering through the windshield.

"You guys came back for us," she whispered.

They'd only been five minutes away when she'd called.

"Of course," Helen said softly. "You would've done the same."

"Plane is still here," Otto exclaimed, excited. He clapped his hands together from where he sat next to Forester.

Ahead, through the windshield of the van, Artemis spotted the small, private airfield and the single plane waiting for them.

On it, new identities. New documents. Hair dye, new clothing. All of it.

Otto was smiling so widely, she thought he might pull a muscle in his cheek.

Helen looked towards the plane with a far-off quality to her gaze.

Artemis was just happy to be on the move again with everyone she loved.

Cameron was alive.

She kept checking to make sure this was true.

They were free.

"You remembered to check in with the coroner, right?" she said, shooting a quick glance back to the driver.

He nodded quickly.

"You have to file the paperwork for cremation. No one can know."

Another quick nod.

Otto leaned in, glaring at the man, and placing a hand on his arm. Otto gave a faint squeeze. "Don't cross us. We've paid you well. Now make her disappear. Are we clear?"

Another, far more frightened nod.

Helen swallowed. "What if Agent Grant doesn't buy it? She seems smart from what you've said."

"She might not," Artemis replied. "But as long as she has some doubts... that might be all we need."

"How much did these new identities cost," Helen asked.

"Cok pahali," the driver replied.

Artemis nodded. "What he said."

The car came to a stop on the airfield. At any moment, Artemis expected the wail of sirens—cars to come up behind them, lights flashing.

But no one came.

No one stopped them.

"Where are we going?" she said.

Her father shook his head. "I'll tell you when we get there." He gave a half glance towards the driver. "The fewer people that know, the better."

Artemis sighed. Forester groaned as he tried to pull open the door. Helen hurried forward, rising from her seat to help him. The door opened. Between Artemis and Helen, Forester disembarked from the van.

Otto came behind them.

The four of them slowly, limping together, approached the waiting plane.

No gunshots.

No sirens.

No shouts of 'you're under arrest!'

Just clear skies above and a plane waiting on the cold tarmac.

For a brief moment, Artemis felt a flutter of... relief? Excitement?

Hope?

She didn't know what was in store. Nor did she know the location her father had chosen.

Would it be somewhere lowkey?

Death always seemed to follow, but a part of her wondered if this was simply the way of it.

Perhaps death didn't follow so much... as she spotted it more readily.

She'd once heard that when someone purchased a blue car, all other blue cars become apparent on the road. The phenomena would convince the person that a sudden crop of blue cars had suddenly emerged...

In reality, their perspective had changed.

And now...

Artemis sighed, approaching the plane.

The front door swung open and she stared.

A figure stood there. A figure she hadn't been expecting.

"Tommy?" she whispered.

"Hop in, sis," he called back.

The youngest Blythe child had pulled his hair back into a pony-tail, but he was still wearing biker leathers. He gestured at them. "Hurry up. Gotta go. Now."

Artemis stared at her brother.

"What?" he said.

"You... you came?"

"Shit. Got in some trouble back home. Now come on! We need'a go."

She nodded, helping Forester forward as the large man winced and grunted.

She glanced around at her father, at Helen, at Tommy... at Cameron.

She allowed herself a small smile.

And to her surprise, she found she meant it.

She didn't know where they were going, what was in store, or what her brother was now running from...

But at least, for once, they were all together. And free.

What's Next for Artemis Blythe?

Old mobsters have old secrets, but they all bleed the same...

Artemis and her family are on the run in Venice, Italy.

With the FBI hot on their trail and an unknown assailant after her brother, Tommy, the family must keep a low profile and lay low. But when Artemis finds herself embroiled in a murder mystery surrounding retired mobsters, the stakes become even higher.

As Tommy searches for a way to clear his name and remove the bounty on his head, Artemis must navigate the dangerous world of organized crime to uncover the truth. Will they be able to stay alive long enough to solve the mystery and save Tommy? Or will they become the next victims in this deadly game? Find out in this thrilling tale of danger, family, and secrets.

ALSO BY GEORGIA WAGNER

A cold knife, a brutal laugh.

Then the odds-defying escape.

Once a hypnotist with her own TV show, now, Sophie Quinn works as a full-time consultant for the FBI. Everything changed six years ago. She can still remember that horrible night. Slated to be the River Killer's tenth victim, she managed to slip her

bindings and barely escape where so many others failed. Her
sister wasn't so lucky.

And now the killer is back.

Two PHDs later, she's now a rising star at the FBI. Her photo-
graphic memory helps solve crimes, but also helps her to never
forget. She saw the River Killer's tattoo. She knows what he
sounds like. And now, ten years later, he's active again.

Sophie Quinn heads back home to the swamps of Louisiana,
along the Mississippi River, intent on evening the score and
finding the man who killed her sister. It's been six years since
she's been home, though. Broken relationships and shattered
dreams exist among the bayous, the rivers, the waterways and
swamps of Louisiana; can Sophie find her way home again? Or
will she be the River Killer's next victim to float downstream?

ALSO BY GEORGIA WAGNER

Once a rising star in the FBI, with the best case closure
rate of any investigator, Ella Porter is now exiled to a small
gold mining town bordering the wilderness of Alaska.
The reason for her new assignment? She allowed a prolific
serial killer to escape custody.

But what no one knows is that she did it on purpose.

The day she shows up in Nome, bags still unpacked, the wife of the richest gold miner in town goes missing. This is the second woman to vanish in as many days. And it's up to Ella to find out what happened.

Assigning Ella to Nome is no accident, either. Though she swore she'd never return, Ella grew up in the small, gold mining town, treated like royalty as a child due to her own family's wealth. But like all gold tycoons, the Porter family secrets are as dark as Ella's own.

Want to know more?

Greenfield press is the brainchild of bestselling author Steve Higgs. He specializes in writing fast paced adventurous mystery and urban fantasy with a humorous lilt. Having made his money publishing his own work, Steve went looking for a few 'special' authors whose work he believed in.

Georgia Wagner was the first of those, but to find out more and to be the first to hear about new releases and what is coming next, you can join the Facebook group by copying the following link into your browser - www.facebook.com/GreenfieldPress.

ABOUT THE AUTHOR

GEORGIA WAGNER WORKED AS a ghost writer for many, many years before finally taking the plunge into self-publishing. Location and character are two big factors for Georgia, and getting those right allows the story to flow seamlessly onto the page. And flow it does, because Georgia is so prolific a new term is required to describe the rate at which nerve-tingling stories find their way into print.

When not found attached to a laptop, Georgia likes spending time in local arboretums, among the trees and ponds. An avid cultivator of orchids, begonias, and all things floral, Georgia also has a strong penchant for art, paintings, and sculptures. A many-decades long passion for mystery novels and years of chess tournament experience makes Georgia the perfect person to pen the Artemis Blythe series.

Printed in Great Britain
by Amazon